"Please let me go," she whispered

At that moment Gay seemed to have no weapons to fight him with.

Luke shook his head. "Not yet," he said thickly.

Their eyes fused until hers fell helplessly. Then they were close, blending together, Luke's mouth against her own in a kiss like none other. Wordlessly they clung together, his hands holding her prisoner.

Gay felt hypnotized, her head spinning as a reckless feeling of pleasure swamped her ability to think.

Then suddenly, with a cruel abruptness Luke pulled away. But Gay was so dazed that she didn't feel the full weight of his rejection until he spoke.

Drawing firmly back he said curtly, "It won't work, Gay. The sooner I get back to London and out of your life the better."

MARGARET PARGETER
is also the author of these

Harlequin Romances

1899—WINDS FROM THE SEA
1951—RIDE A BLACK HORSE
1973—THE KILTED STRANGER
2022—HOLD ME CAPTIVE
2058—BLUE SKIES, DARK WATERS
2112—NEVER GO BACK
2140—FLAMINGO MOON
2168—WILD INHERITANCE
2183—BETTER TO FORGET
2193—MIDNIGHT MAGIC
2211—THE JEWELLED CAFTAN
2227—THE WILD ROWAN
2241—A MAN CALLED CAMERON
2260—MARRIAGE IMPOSSIBLE
2284—ONLY YOU
2296—THE DEVIL'S BRIDE
2350—AUTUMN SONG
2375—KISS OF A TYRANT
2409—DARK SURRENDER
2416—DECEPTION
2422—CAPTIVITY

and these

Harlequin Presents

145—STORMY RAPTURE
366—SAVAGE POSSESSION
431—THE DARK OASIS
453—BOOMERANG BRIDE

At First Glance

by

MARGARET PARGETER

Harlequin Books

TORONTO • LONDON • LOS ANGELES • AMSTERDAM
SYDNEY • HAMBURG • PARIS • STOCKHOLM • ATHENS • TOKYO

Original hardcover edition published in 1981
by Mills & Boon Limited

ISBN 0-373-02475-4

Harlequin edition published May 1982

Printed in U.S.A.

CHAPTER ONE

THE telephone rang and with a sigh Gay Fenton picked it up, giving her number. Vaguely she hoped it wasn't for her. She'd had a long day and wasn't feeling particularly sociable.

'Is that you, Gay?'

Resignedly Gay confirmed that it was. She recognised Katrina's voice instantly. That wasn't surprising as Katrina and she had been reared in the same town and gone to the same schools, their families having been friends for generations. Katrina had even married a distant relation of the Fentons, one David Douglas. She was, though, several years older than Gay, who wasn't yet twenty.

'I'm in a jam, darling. Could you possibly help me?' Katrina's voice was unusually anxious.

'Tell me what it is first, then I'll decide,' Gay replied cautiously.

Katrina obliged, with a haste that warned Gay that she must indeed be anxious about something. 'It's David, darling. The silly man has gone and asked his boss to dinner. Which would have been bad enough,' she added, 'what with the kids and the dog and everything, but he's had the nerve to ask if he can bring his aunt as well.'

'Whose aunt?' Gay interrupted uncertainly.

'David's boss's aunt, of course!' Katrina sounded taut with impatience. 'Are you being deliberately dense, Gay? You must know David doesn't have an aunt, at least, not a proper one.'

Wryly Gay quirked her feathery brows. 'Maybe I'm just naturally dense, Katrina, because I can't see what any of this has to do with me.'

'I'll explain,' Katrina cried, 'if you'll just give me a minute! If it hadn't been for the dratted aunt, I might have coped, but how can David possibly expect me to be rushing in and out of the kitchen, serving dinner, while at the same time trying to make intelligent, entertaining conversation with the kind of people who will expect it?'

'Why don't you get in touch with one of those firms who do it all for you?' Gay suggested quickly, as Katrina paused for breath. She could have told Katrina to calm down, but that would simply have been a waste of time.

'Don't be silly!' Katrina rushed on. 'It would cost the earth. And at the moment, just one more thing would have David's bank manager screaming down his neck. Besides,' she added, on a note of extreme exasperation, which hinted coldly that Gay shouldn't have to be told these things, 'how would hired caterers cope with a fretful two-year-old and a baby who refuses to sleep?'

'You do seem to be having problems,' Gay agreed soothingly, trying to forget she had plenty of her own. 'Don't you think, though, that you're taking it all a bit too seriously?'

Katrina almost wept down the phone. 'I wouldn't be taking it seriously at all if it weren't so important. You see, David's chances of promotion apparently rest with me. It seems Mr Ashley believes the right kind of wife is very important. In other words, the impression I make could make all the difference between success and failure, so far as David's concerned. And if David doesn't get this new position he's after, it will mean disaster for both of us!'

Gay frowned, imagining Katrina was alluding to the financial difficulties which always seemed to be with her. 'I thought David had already been promoted?'

'No, silly. We're only here for six months, while the permanent man's doing a stint abroad. But, if the evening I'm talking about is a success, David is pretty sure he'll be offered a job in London, at head office.'

'I didn't know David knew anyone as exalted as the managing director. You always said he had no hope of meeting him.'

'Well, Luke Ashley is Ashley Industries, and you must know what that means, even in these hard times. David's only got to know him because Mr Ashley has just bought a house in the neighbourhood, and because of this—or we *think* because of this, has started taking a more personal interest in the local factory complex.'

'Does he live near you?' Gay asked indifferently.

'A few miles out of town. I haven't seen the house, but it's reputed to be gorgeous. Even the sound of it makes me feel quite green with envy.'

Gay wasn't really curious, but she found herself enquiring, 'What made him settle there, I wonder? His wife?'

'His aunt, I believe. She was born in these parts, seemingly. David doesn't think he has a wife. At least he hasn't heard of one.'

'Well,' Gay smothered a yawn, 'where do I come in? You did say you wanted to ask me something?'

'Ask you to do something, was what I meant,' Katrina explained hurriedly. 'Yes, I wanted to ask if you would come and be my maid for the evening?'

'Maid?' Gay whispered incredulously. 'Katrina, you must be joking! Not,' she added hastily, 'that I've anything against maids—I haven't. But I wouldn't know where to start.'

'Of course you would!' Katrina snapped, forgetting she had intended being cajoling. 'You're a superb cook and there can't be much about dinner parties you don't know. Your parents entertain enough.'

Feeling slightly stunned, Gay ignored this. 'Couldn't I come as a guest? I could still assist.'

'No!' Katrina wailed. 'I mean, it wouldn't give the same impression, would it? David says Luke Ashley is terribly high class, so his aunt's probably worse—women always are. What would they think if I had another guest jumping up and down all the time, helping serve the potatoes? As a maid you'd be ideal,' she enthused. 'Not only would it look good, but the kids know you.'

Which implied, Gay had no doubt, that she'd have them to deal with as well, should they decide to play up. She grinned suddenly to herself. Two little darlings, but rascals, always seeming to be making a row. In some ways she could sympathise with Katrina.

Katrina had another surprise in store. 'I was going to ask you to come down anyway, next weekend, as David and I have to go to a wedding up north. We'll only be away one night, but there's no one here we know well enough to look after the children, and we can't take them with us.'

'No, that's understandable,' Gay laughed with half-hearted humour. 'I hope you can supply the energy I'm apparently going to need!'

'Does that mean you'll come?' asked Katrina eagerly.

'Am I allowed to refuse?' Gay quipped dryly. 'If I tried you'd only talk me into it somehow, so I suppose it's no use saying that I think you're slightly mad. Just one thing, though,' she felt compelled to ask, 'what if someone were to recognise me and give the game away?'

'Really, Gay, the expressions you use!' Katrina's tone was disapproving, now she'd got her own way. 'There's no fear of anything like that happening. You've only been here once or twice on short visits and neither times do I recall you meeting anyone.'

'Well,' said Gay, 'it was only a thought.'

'If anything like that were to happen, I'll simply say there must have been some mistake.'

'And what will you tell the Ashleys when I suddenly disappear?' Gay asked sweetly. 'After all, if David isn't promoted and you're stuck where you are, you might easily be seeing them again.'

'How reassuring you are!' Katrina muttered acidly.

'If the Ashleys did happen to notice I don't have a maid any more, I'll simply drag out the usual twaddle about staff problems. That might sound too starchy, but I'll think of something,' she promised, with her first hint of humour.

'It won't be my worry,' Gay returned smoothly, yet feeling quite concerned, all the same.

'But you will come?' Katrina demanded confirmation anxiously.

'If you like,' Gay sighed. 'I haven't anything much better to do, I suppose. I'm only working Tuesdays, Wednesdays and Thursdays. Spilling soup down the neck of one of the country's most influential men might make a nice change!'

'You wouldn't!'

'Oh, all right,' Gay relented. 'Cheer up. I should think I'll be able to do the job with my eyes closed.' As Katrina groaned aloud again, she promised rashly, 'Stop worrying, I'll come early on Friday and cook the whole meal myself. How about that?' As Katrina breathed fervent thanks, she added, 'I'll try to think of something which will almost guarantee David's promotion.'

The following Friday, true to her word, Gay caught an early train. The early train mightn't have been absolutely essential, but she was glad to get away from the flat. Morris, Gay's half-brother, had been in a foul mood the night before. He was a photographer, quite a famous one, and Gay lived with him while their parents were abroad. Six months ago it had seemed an ideal arrangement, as otherwise it would have meant running a large house just for one, as well as Gay having to live alone.

Morris, absorbed in his work, had agreed to have his sister without giving the matter much thought. However, being much older than Gay, he soon found her presence restrictive. Her innocence alone prevented him bringing to the flat the kind of women he occasionally liked to entertain. Now he felt forced to make do with brief affairs conducted outside, or during clandestine weekends in hotels, and even this could make him feel guilty, a feeling he didn't altogether appreciate.

Gay, not quite so unaware of the facts of life as Morris imagined, was more conscious of the situation than he guessed. One of the models who worked for him had been to the flat a lot lately and Gay suspected that Morris would sometimes have liked her to stay. Tactfully Gay had tried to occupy herself elsewhere in the evenings, when she knew Julie was there. But last night she had felt terribly embarrassed when, on returning home, she had practically bumped into Julie emerging from Morris's bedroom, clad only in a thin negligee. Morris had laughed and declared they were simply catching up on some work, but Gay had sensed his extreme irritation.

Then there was the problem of Gay's own career. For three days a week she worked for a friend who ran her own boutique. On other days she helped Morris with his accounts and typing, but this was only until she decided what she really wanted to do. Morris would have liked her to model for him, yet, contrarily, was reluctant to involve her in what he cynically declared was usually one of the most hazardous ways of earning a living. Their parents, though, wouldn't hear of it, for all Morris insisted perversely that Gay's face was one of the most photogenic he had ever seen. Meanwhile, as Gay herself had no desire to become a model, nothing had come of it. Yet, as she gazed from the train window on bleak March landscapes, Gay realised she couldn't remain with her brother indefinitely. One of these days she must seriously consider launching out on her own.

The station being a few miles from where Katrina and David actually lived necessitated the catching of a bus. Taxis were available, but Gay didn't consider herself in that much of a hurry. Besides, to go by bus would save money.

About ten yards from the bus stop a superb car drew

up beside her. Frowning, Gay wondered if she must still be half asleep because of her early start, as surely she had seen the same, very noticeable vehicle passing in the opposite direction.

A rather striking-looking man leaned out and asked coolly, 'Going some place?'

Startled, she paused, her frown deepening, as something in his eyes caught and held her own, making her shiver. More alarmingly, he didn't seem in any hurry to release her gaze, and a peculiar sensation lanced the pit of her stomach. It was indescribable, and crazily, it seemed to hurt.

Go away, she almost cried, as mysterious pinpricks tore through her. Instead she heard herself murmuring in confusion, 'Yes. Yes, I am.'

'I thought you wouldn't be out sightseeing,' the man smiled.

'Hardly, on a day like this,' she retorted, recovering her composure and dismissing her disturbing symptoms as purely imaginary.

Without further ado the stranger flung open the door on Gay's side. 'Hop in, then,' he commanded, clearly used to giving orders, his eyes, keenly assessing, never leaving her face. With her fluffy red hair blowing wildly about her elegant little head which emerged on a slender, graceful neck from the depth of her white fur coat, she looked wholly young and enchanting.

When he repeated his offer, framed slightly more conventionally, Gay was amazed to hear herself saying, 'Yes . . . Why not?'

If she had subconsciously hoped to confound him by her swift acceptance of an offer which all well brought up girls were expected to refuse, there was nothing in the man's aggressively masculine face to suggest he was shocked in any way. Gay was left feeling slightly deflated, wondering at her own boldness. Never before had she entered a strange car or had anything to do with a man she hadn't been properly introduced to. It must be the feelings this man aroused in her which were making her so reckless. Yet she was startled that she was allowing him to affect her so. As she sat beside him, she hoped nervously that by enduring his company for a few minutes she might soon get back to normal. The area was built up. She was perfectly safe. If he tried anything she would soon let him see she was more than capable of taking care of herself.

'Where do you want to go?'

His voice was smooth and well modulated, but instead of soothing her nerves it appeared to make them worse. The tingling began again, forcing her to draw a steadying breath. 'Brockfield. Do you know it?'

'I believe so. That's the older part of the town, isn't it?' As she nodded, he asked, 'Which street?'

Slightly cautious, she replied, 'The estate will do.'

He wasn't so easily put off. 'It's just as easy to drop you at the right spot.'

Gay hesitated and swallowed. She remembered a house which she had mistaken for Katrina's and David's, the first time she had come here. Confused as to why she didn't want this man to know her exact destination, she muttered untruthfully, 'The street's called Hathaway. I'd be much obliged if you'd put me down at the end of it.'

With a nod he switched the ignition and the car slid silently from the kerb. 'Do you live here or are you just visiting?' he asked.

'Neither,' she replied briefly, shooting an anxious glance at his strong profile.

'Do I have to guess all the way?' he asked dryly, his lean hands tightening with obvious irritation on the steering wheel. Disconcerted, she sensed the power in those long, steely fingers.

That summed him up, Gay thought irrationally, jerking her gaze in front again. He was a man who was powerful right through, a stranger to any kind of weakness. Suddenly such infallibility was frightening and she felt herself tremble. 'Whether I live here or not doesn't matter,' she gulped. 'It was good of you to give me a lift, but would you please stop now and let me out. This will do nicely.'

'As I said,' he insisted, 'it's no more trouble to drop you off at the right place.' As though sensing her agitation, he slowed to a determined crawl. 'This may seem sudden, but I'd like to see you again. Would you have dinner with me?'

'No!' She could feel her cheeks going pink, her limbs shaking. Amazingly they felt so weak she doubted if they would immediately support her. 'I might have been foolish to accept a lift, but I do have some sense. Besides,' she added, without knowing why, 'I'm not free this evening.'

'Neither am I, unfortunately.'

As he muttered the words impatiently, Gay pointed impulsively to a vacant space beside a house that looked deserted. 'Over there, if you don't mind.'

Expertly he edged into the pavement and parked. Turning to her, he caught her arm, persisting softly, 'I understand how you feel—but lunch with me today? Then we can get to know each other better and make arrangements for tomorrow.'

Disbelievingly incredulous, Gay lifted startled eyes to stare at him, and was again panicky at the electrical effect when their eyes met. Her heart raced and she was lost in the silvery glitter of his glance. Every bit of her seemed to tighten and tingle alarmingly. 'You're enjoying yourself at my expense,' she whispered helplessly.

'No,' he shook his dark head with a slight smile, 'I'm simply asking you to enjoy yourself at mine.'

'Very funny!' she gasped. 'I don't even know you.'

'I've already suggested we rectify that.'

She tried to protest, but his other hand came out to touch her creamy cheek and she seemed to lose the ability to utter even a single sound.

The weighted purpose in his voice alarmed her as he

drew nearer. 'You're very beautiful,' his fingers explored her delicate features. 'You'll have to excuse me—this is the first time I've ever done anything like this, but I never thought to find anything quite so perfect.'

Gay couldn't have moved had she tried. His hand cupped her chin, tilting her face towards him, his eyes intent as though mesmerised, on her unsteady lips. Then his head dropped, and, as if she had issued a silent invitation, his hovering mouth touched her own. What happened next was for Gay indescribable. She had been conscious of something between them, bringing them irrevocably together, but as his hard mouth pressed over hers, she felt drawn up in timeless space, all her strength taken from her, then flung insensibly into a whirling vortex of passion and desire.

The sensation could only have been momentary, for, like a ravaging predator scenting danger, the stranger withdrew. Dazed though she was, he reminded Gay of a man suddenly caught in a swamp and warily determined not to sink any farther. Caution was replacing the former blaze in his eyes, while his mouth, which only moments ago had been seeking hers sensuously, went curiously taut. Instantly she knew he was questioning his own sanity and pulled angrily away from him.

'Wait a minute,' he begged huskily, a curious indecision in his eyes which Gay guessed wasn't normal. 'Let me introduce myself. We seem to have started off on the wrong foot. My name is . . .'

'Oh, please, I don't want to know!' she choked wildly, wanting only to escape his hateful presence. Reaching for the door, she was thankful when it opened at first touch, letting her tumble clumsily out on to the street. Hastily she stumbled away from the car, rushing blindly up the path of a strange semi-detached, praying no one was at home. If anyone was she would have to pretend she was lost, but she wasn't sure what she would say if the man followed her. She supposed she could always appeal to the people who lived there—if the house was occupied—for help, but she felt oddly reluctant to do so. As she fled around the back of the house, however, she soon realised she wasn't being pursued, and knew a great surge of relief on hearing the car drive away.

Grateful that a kinder fate had at last decided to take a hand, Gay turned quickly and went back to the road. Her relief now seemed mixed with a peculiar disappointment when she saw the stranger had indeed gone. He certainly gave up easily, considering how eager he had been for her company, she told herself irrationally. Then, surprised at her own thoughts, she rebuked herself firmly. Wasn't it just as well? He was attractive, granted, but decidedly not her sort. A man of his age and type—she guessed him a business man of some sort, in his thirties—could only have been amusing himself. Perhaps she should count herself fortunate that he had lost interest so quickly.

Holding fast to her angry indignation, Gay hurried rather furtively from the vicinity of the house where she had sought refuge. It was highly unlikely the man would return and embarrass the occupants by demanding to see a girl who didn't live there. But if he did there was nothing she could do about it.

As she swiftly completed the remaining half mile, to the correct address this time, she was bewildered to find her thoughts clinging to the stranger. She was sure he wasn't the kind of man who usually picked girls up. While she pondered over this quite a lot, she refused to remember how she had felt when he had kissed her. For a laugh she would relate the whole episode to Katrina, who always enjoyed a good joke. It consequently confused Gay that she didn't mention it at all, especially as it wasn't until after lunch that the shaky feeling left her legs and she felt nearly herself again. Pushing what had happened to the back of her mind, she did her utmost to forget it.

Just after seven, she patted the white starched cap on

her head, viewing her neat reflection in the kitchen mirror with some satisfaction. A uniform could look very attractive, she thought, forgetting that like everything else it depended on who was wearing it.

Behind her, Katrina sighed fretfully and Gay turned on her impatiently. 'I wish you'd stop worrying, Katrina. It's not as if we're committing a crime! You're simply pretending to have a maid for an evening, and it's a bit late now to change your mind. You'd never get anyone else at the last minute and we both know you couldn't possibly manage everything on your own. Not when you're entertaining royalty!'

'Oh, don't be silly,' Katrina cried, not prepared to find anything even faintly humorous in the situation. 'They aren't royalty, I mean.'

'Perhaps it's a pity,' Gay rejoined dryly. 'If they had been I don't think you'd be half as scared as you are now. David's boss and his aunt can't be that frightening.'

'Of course not,' Katrina agreed, too emphatically. 'It's just that—well, so much depends on this visit, doesn't it? David's promotion might be a giggle to you, but for us it means everything.'

'You seem very comfortable as you are,' Gay pointed out mildly.

'Is that another way of saying you don't know why we bother?' Katrina asked coldly. 'Haven't you noticed how shabby the hall carpet is? It won't stand more than a forty-watt bulb. Then there's the children and their clothes, to say nothing of their education! Oh, I realise they aren't old enough, but they soon will be. Soon there'll be school fees and uniforms . . .'

'I can't see what's wrong with the good old comprehensive,' Gay sighed.

'You wouldn't, would you!' Katrina retorted sharply, 'seeing how you always had the best . . .'

'A lot of good it's done me,' Gay brooded. 'It hasn't helped me discover what I want to do with my life. All I have at the moment is a part-time job and no prospects. As well as no proper ambitions,' she added darkly.

'It wouldn't have been so bad,' Katrina frowned, dismissing Gay's troubles as of no account, compared to the size of her own, 'if the aunt hadn't been coming.'

'Why does Mr Ashley want to bring her, do you know?'

'She's new to the neighbourhood and lonely, I believe,' Katrina shrugged. 'David says she wants to get to know people.'

'But you might be moving, so she could be wasting her time.'

'Not if David doesn't get this higher position he's after, we won't.'

'This house is very cosy,' Gay glanced around the large, old-fashioned kitchen appreciatively. 'Give me space every time.'

'You wouldn't say that if you had to keep it clean. With no permanent help,' Katrina grinned suddenly.

'Well,' Gay laughed, her own face lighting up, 'you have got help, for the next few hours, at least, so cheer up.'

'I don't think I fully realised what I was taking on.' Katrina's smile faded, as she viewed Gay's slim figure dubiously.

'Just because I've never actually been a maid, it doesn't necessarily mean I'm going to make a lot of mistakes,' Gay said impatiently. 'If I do you can always blame it on my youth. No one expects much of young people nowadays.'

'It's not that funny!' Katrina's brown eyes hardened with exasperation. 'You might just be nineteen, but I'm a good six years older. Old enough to have known better.'

Gay paused, concentrating on a noise outside. 'It's too late now,' she almost smiled with relief, 'I think I hear a car.'

'Oh, that'll be them!' Katrina exclaimed frantically,

and with an indignant glance at Gay's calm face, fled from the kitchen.

After she had gone, Gay sat down thankfully. Poor Katrina! She should never have married an up-and-coming young executive with a yen to get on. While Katrina had ambitions, they were entirely wrapped up in her home and family. She hated outside involvement. David was all right; he knew where he was going. He didn't panic as Katrina did. This evening, though, he did seem rather on edge, so perhaps this dinner was important.

Gay didn't hold with the popular concept that a wife must prove herself sociably acceptable before her husband could be allowed anyway near the top of the ladder. Yet David, surprisingly, didn't agree with her. An international giant like Ashleys, he insisted, could afford to be particular. That Luke Ashley had accepted an invitation to dinner was, he appeared to believe, an honour in itself.

Idly Gay wondered what Luke Ashley could be looking for. Katrina was a nice girl, if inclined to be a little dithery. He wouldn't find much to fault there. Possibly he wouldn't be looking for anything specially. With his experience he could probably sum people up in seconds.

Be that as it may, Gay didn't like the idea of any industrial tycoon mentally stripping Katrina down to the basics. No doubt he would concentrate on her faults rather than her virtues. Indignantly, Gay patted the head of David's old dog, who growled his objections.

'Sorry, Ben,' she murmured.

As he wagged his forgiveness, David popped into the kitchen. 'Now don't go doing anything silly, Gay,' he warned, as if he sensed her mood wasn't quite what it should be.

'I won't,' she promised wryly.

Still frowning, he stared at her. 'Katrina must have been mad to have dreamt this up in the first place!'

'She often acts on impulse,' Gay soothed.

'Something which would scarcely recommend her to Mr Ashley.'

'Oh, bother Mr Ashley!' Gay retorted sharply. 'Anyway, it's too late now to have second thoughts. Aren't they already here? I thought I heard a car.'

'That was just the chap down the road, come to borrow the spanner he borrowed and failed to return last week,' he said dryly.

'There's another car now, though,' Gay held up a cautioning finger, adding quietly, 'It mightn't be someone else this time.'

As the doorbell rang, David's nice-looking face creased anxiously. 'You will be careful, Gay, won't you? If Mr Ashley ever learns the truth of this, I'll only go one way, and that's out!'

'You're exaggerating!' Gay laughed, even as she nodded. She was unable to take it all so seriously, though she did feel a twinge of misgiving. This must be David's fault, for going on so!

'Don't forget,' he warned again, with the air of a man forced to make the best of things, 'give us half an hour, then announce dinner.'

Biting her lip, Gay went to peer in the oven. Everything was coming along nicely. At least there was nothing to worry about there. It must be the right car this time as in the background she could hear the murmur of voices, then the sound of the lounge door opening and closing. They had decided it might seem a little too ostentatious to have Gay showing the guests in, although she had offered. David was also seeing to the drinks himself, so as, he'd said cautiously, to keep Gay out of sight as much as possible.

Gay wrinkled her slightly retroussé nose. If Luke Ashley ever did find out she wasn't really the maid, she would make darned sure—if he had the nerve to complain—that he realised the Douglases could never afford proper help on what he paid them!

Feeling better, she stirred the consommé with greater

confidence. It was her favourite recipe and if David had helped himself to much more there shouldn't have been any left. The entrée, a delectable concoction, again of her own devising, was already on the table, along with fruit juice for anyone who preferred it. While the Douglases and their guests consumed this and the soup, she would get the main course ready to serve.

Half an hour later exactly, Gay again patted her starched white cap in place. Together with the white pinafore which she wore over one of Katrina's summer cottons, she thought she looked very properly attired. Katrina was a size larger than Gay, so the blue dress was on the big side, but not enough to be noticeable. If anything, it increased her air of incredible fragility.

Katrina had frowned over this. Gay, she had declared, with her soft red hair and violet blue eyes, looked nothing like a maid—at least, not the kind of maid she'd had in mind. She was too slender, too curvy, even her long, slim legs seemed all wrong. It wasn't until Gay's hair had been tucked completely out of sight under her cap that Katrina had been satisfied.

Suddenly, as Gay stared at her severe, nunlike reflection, she was beset by the same uncertainty that afflicted Katrina and David. Firmly she told herself not to be so silly, yet it took more willpower than she thought possible to get from the kitchen to the lounge. Knocking quietly on the door, she opened it, announcing in her most sedate voice that dinner was served. Keeping her eyes nervously fixed on the floor, she was only conscious of the brief silence which greeted her words, nothing more.

When David cleared his throat and murmured, 'Thank you, Gay,' she retreated rather quickly. Feeling her legs shaking, she was tempted to rest on the chair in the hall, but remembered just in time that the Ashleys might think it odd. It astonished her that she should feel so strange. Funnily enough, it was a feeling not so unlike that which she had experienced in the car of the man who had given her a lift that morning. What ever it was, it made her go quite weak at the knees. Anxiously she hoped she wasn't sickening for something.

Hurrying to the dining-room, she stood meekly to one side as the company entered and David organised the seating. She was supposed to help, but her legs were playing her up again and incredibly she seemed unable to move. This bewildering sensation continued to puzzle her—until she lifted her head to meet the cool gaze of a pair of silvery grey eyes.

The ensuing shock was so great, for a few seconds Gay was consumed by it. Helplessly she dropped the folded napkin she was carrying and had to bend to pick it up. All the time as she did so she was aware of being watched expressionlessly by the man who must be David's boss.

As she straightened, she forced herself to look at him again. Her glance was apprehensively brief, but she saw enough to convince her it really was the same man she had encountered that morning. Then he had worn a high-necked sweater under a bulky fur coat which, somehow, had made him appear slightly foreign. Now he wore a plain dark suit which accentuated his undeniable attractiveness just as much, if a little differently. This evening he had a kind of dark distinction which made her quiver. He looked coldly remote, a man who weighed every move and never acted on impulse. She could find nothing in his face of the harsh passion which had driven him so unexpectedly to kiss her. Nothing, in fact, that betrayed in any way that he knew her, or why he had acted as he had done that morning.

CHAPTER TWO

NERVOUSLY, as she went about her various duties, Gay's eyes kept returning to Luke Ashley's face. Surprisingly he continued staring at her just as intently as she stared at him, while no one else appeared to notice. Suddenly aware of how intimately she was detailing his every feature, she was relieved when Katrina warned her that they were almost ready for the next course.

That this man was Luke Ashley was unfortunate, but, Gay reassured herself, it was just possible he didn't recognise her. And even if he did, she didn't think he would hold David responsible for his maid's behaviour. It was more likely, if he did recognise her, that he was thanking his lucky stars she had refused to go out with him that morning. He wasn't the sort, she decided, with an inward shrug of amusement, to take a girl who did domestic work out to dinner. Perhaps it was just as well she hadn't known he was the great Mr Ashley, otherwise she might have been tempted to accept his invitation. It might have been worth it to have been able to watch his embarrassment when he learnt who she really was.

It wasn't until she was serving the consommé and he turned to speak to Katrina that Gay suddenly remembered she wasn't actually a maid, and such a joke could only have rebounded eventually on herself. She must be going slightly mad, she thought, again aware of Luke Ashley's glinting glance. She suspected he was attempting to turn two very different girls into the same one. Instinctively she feared, as she returned to the kitchen, that this was absorbing him more than David's future promotion, or the suitability of his wife.

As she placed a warm plate before him, so he could help himself to the duck casserole, her hands trembled.

And when he stared straight up at her with a murmur of thanks, the trembling ran right up her arm and inside her body. It must be sheer nervousness, but she couldn't recall feeling this way before. She felt curious and a little alarmed that any man could affect her so.

By the time she served coffee the meal was an acknowledged success, which surprisingly did little for the taut state of Gay's nerves. One awkward moment had been survived when Luke Ashley's aunt had asked Katrina the secret of her delicious casserole. Fortunately, after a barely perceptible hesitation, during which Gay held her breath, Katrina had stammered that it was rather complicated and it might be better if she wrote the recipe out later.

As if aware of Gay's relief when Miss Ashley said this would do nicely, David rashly glanced at Gay and winked. Unhappily Gay sensed someone had witnessed this, and her fears proved correct. When her eyes swivelled swiftly to Luke Ashley, it was to find him glancing narrowly from David to herself, a flicker of quick contempt on his face. What actual construction he was placing on David's easy but innocent familiarity, she shuddered to think. David, she fumed, should have known better! Yet somehow she couldn't condemn him as angrily as she did Luke Ashley, for jumping so quickly to the wrong conclusions.

Once dinner was over, Gay was thankful she needn't appear again until it was time to fetch the visitors' coats. The kitchen, warm and quiet, was like a haven after a storm. She even welcomed the pile of dishes waiting to be washed. It would be easier to concentrate on these rather than her own too troublesome thoughts.

Having washed the cutlery, she was just about to begin on the rest when she heard a warning whimper from the nursery, which was directly above her. It would be Nigel, the baby. Shooting upstairs, drying her hands on a towel as she went, she hurriedly snatched him from his cot before he managed to disturb the entire household. Young Nigel, not being a placid baby, refused to be comforted and, as he was wet, she decided to take him down to the kitchen and change him there.

After this was accomplished, Gay began rocking him in her arms and was pleased when he snuggled against her with an angelic little smile. Soon he was asleep again. She was just about to return him to his room when the door opened and, to her dismay, Luke Ashley walked in.

Startled, she stared at him, clutching the baby so tightly she almost woke him up. She had to swallow twice in an effort to find her voice. Consequently Luke Ashley beat her to it.

'I'd like a drink of water, if I may?' Closing the door, he walked slowly towards the sink, without once taking his eyes from her face.

'Yes. Oh, of course.' Awkwardly she tried to open a cupboard to extract a glass, but pushing her gently aside he got one for himself.

Slanting her a quick glance, he turned on the cold tap, holding the glass underneath it. Suddenly she had an awful suspicion he wasn't even thirsty, that his trip to the kitchen had been made simply to satisfy his curiosity. She resolved not to accuse him of this, however, as, if he admitted she was right, she wasn't sure what she could say next.

He made no attempt to claim any previous knowledge of her existence, although she felt in her very bones that he knew exactly who she was. His eyes, which were curiously silver one moment and black the next, played over her. Although they were strangers, Gay was very conscious of the peculiar awareness between them that set her pulses thudding and her senses aflame.

As a faint colour edged its way to her smooth cheeks, he nodded at the sleeping baby. 'Yours?'

Her colour deepening, she thrust back an angry retort, merely shaking her head. For a second she had been tempted to nod and so confirm his obvious opinion that she was no better than she should be. He was basing his conclusions, she suspected, on the indiscreet wink David had thrown her in the dining-room, and, suddenly incensed, she would like to have said something to really shock—even hurt him. It took a lot of effort to restrain herself as cautiously she feared that in seeking such satisfaction she might only succeed in hurting David and Katrina.

'Have you worked here long?' Luke Ashley asked when she didn't speak.

Again she shook her head, but this time feeling forced to be a little more explicit. 'No.'

'Do you intend staying with the Douglases?'

She wished he would go away instead of pestering her with questions she didn't want to answer. 'I'm not sure,' she replied at last, coldly.

'So you have no real intention of settling in these parts?' he rejoined enigmatically.

'I didn't say that.' Her glance strayed to his mouth and she looked quickly away again. It was harsher than she remembered. This morning she hadn't noticed the hint of cruelty. She had felt it, though, when he had kissed her. Swiftly she lowered her betraying eyes for fear he guessed what she was thinking. He would want to be reminded of that incident no more than she. His trip to the kitchen must have been made with the deliberate intention of conveying that he no longer wished to know her. He was a snob, she decided scornfully, having no desire to further their acquaintance herself.

The baby in her arms stirred and she remembered she had been going to take him back upstairs. 'Excuse me,' she murmured, glad of an excuse to escape.

When she returned Luke Ashley had gone. He had left his glass on the table and under it a ten-pound note. Gay gazed at the money incredulously, her heart hammering, her cheeks hot. The beast! How dared he insult her like this! It was meant as an insult, she was certain.

It was his way of trying to ensure that she didn't mention his behaviour this morning to anyone. And that he didn't want anyone to hear of it seemed to speak for itself!

Biting her lip, Gay crumpled the ten-pound note in agitated fingers. She supposed, in a way, she could understand his point of view, but she had thought such snobbery was a thing of the past. Luke Ashley's dinner must almost have choked him after he had seen her and realised the mistake he had made.

Yet she couldn't help feeling that in spite of everything something didn't quite fit. Had he really felt it necessary to come to the kitchen and buy her silence with money? As she had refused to go out with him, wouldn't it have been more natural for him to have ignored the whole matter? If anyone had learnt of it she doubted they would have dared challenge him about it. Plenty of men like him had affairs with all kinds of girls. Maid or no maid, no one might have thought less of him for making a pass at her.

Gay frowned as she got on with the dishes. It was funny how she continued to think of herself as Katrina's maid. It was as if she had suddenly acquired a split personality and refused to let go of this new image. Luke Ashley, she felt sure, had a sense of humour. If she had been honest, explained the whole situation to him, it was more than probable he would have laughed and forgiven her.

So why did she harbour such foolish fancies about being carried off by a knight in shining armour, who didn't give a jot who she was, or what she did for a living? Before this morning such a thought had never crossed her mind and she refused to admit it had anything to do with the arrogant Luke Ashley that she now thought differently. It must be sheer coincidence, possibly because of seeing David and Katrina so happy with the children, that she was beginning to think wistfully of a home and family of her own.

Reminding herself that she had a lot more important things to do before she was ready for that, Gay swept the offensive note from the sink top. She would burn it! Then she hesitated. No, she would keep it and return it to its rightful owner. Somehow, somewhere, she would find an opportunity, and when that day came, she might just see Luke Ashley squirm, even worse than she was doing now.

The following morning found the Douglas household in a not unusual state of chaos. Katrina blamed it on the dinner party and the harassing time she had had trying to find the list of unusual ingredients Gay had demanded for cooking it. Even finding and marinating the ducks had taken a lot of time. Whatever the cause, she found she had forgotten several important items for the baby, so Gay was despatched, not unwillingly, to the chemist's to get them.

She had to walk as David was too busy checking the car to take her. He did promise, if he finished in time, that he would come and pick her up.

'I don't mind walking,' she smiled, thinking David the nicest of cousins. 'It's only half a mile. When you finish it might be better if you gave Katrina a hand with your packing.'

They were setting off for the wedding at eleven and as it was only after nine they ought to be ready. Much as she loved Katrina, Gay felt she wouldn't be sorry to see the last of her for a day or so, at least until she stopped talking so enthusiastically about Luke Ashley. All through breakfast she had gone on about his superb manners and good looks. She had even gone as far as to say that a man like that could make her wish she were single again.

David, having endured his wife's ramblings in silence, eventually retaliated. With a dry frankness he declared that even if Katrina had been single he doubted if it would have done her much good. Luke Ashley was too concerned with making money to involve himself seriously with any girl. And while it was known that he did indulge in an occasional affair, David had heard it whispered, direct from head office, that he thought nothing of cancelling a date with a girl-friend at a moment's notice if something important in the way of business cropped up.

'It needn't be that important, either,' he stiffly warned his dazzled wife. 'He apparently tires very easily of his women friends, especially when they become too demanding. His secretary, I believe, has often to console them over the phone.'

'He might change.' Katrina, this morning, seemed to have completely reversed her former opinion of David's boss. 'I'm surprised someone hasn't already snapped him up. He has a kind of aristocratic distinction, don't you think,' she appealed to Gay, 'as well as being very sexy.'

Gay suppressed a giggle in the face of David's shocked surprise. 'Good God!' he exclaimed. 'Whatever next? I also happen to know,' he continued angrily, obviously thinking Katrina had taken leave of her senses, 'that far from him being of the aristocracy, Mr Ashley's father was working class. Which probably explains,' he concluded, with a mixture of disparagement and envy, 'why his son appears determined to stop at nothing until he's a millionaire several times over.'

Gay tried not to listen, but it had been difficult not to hear what was being said, and neither David or Katrina had seemed to remember she was there. She was glad to escape, even if on nothing more exciting than a trip to the shops. Katrina had obviously fallen victim to Luke Ashley's not inconsiderable charm, but Gay suspected that her trip up north to a wedding might be absorbing enough to make her forget him. If not she felt sorry for poor David who, after five years of marriage, still loved his wife to distraction.

Gay wore her fur coat again as the air was cool. Having little doubt as to where Katrina's real affections lay, she skipped along. It was windy and the wind always did make her feel like dancing. On the return journey, though, she didn't find it possible to do other than walk sedately, owing to the weight of two full shopping bags. Which was why she almost smiled with relief on seeing David turning at the roundabout to pull up beside her. Quickly he put the shopping in the boot, then, placing an absent arm around her shoulders, he turned her towards the passenger door of the car. As he did so he made a laughing remark about his absurd jealousy over Katrina and Luke Ashley.

'Kat and I have been married five years,' he grinned ruefully. 'I love her, but I thought I was long past the stage of hating to hear her praising another man.'

Smiling back, Gay reached up to pat his cheek, teasing affectionately, 'Why don't you give her a nice big kiss when you get home? Then I'm sure she'll never give Mr Ashley another thought.'

'You're a gem, Gay. I might do just that.' David hugged her with light appreciation. 'But talk of the devil!' he muttered darkly.

The dismay in his voice had Gay swinging swiftly around, just in time to see Luke Ashley cruising smoothly past in his smart limousine.

'Do you think he saw us?' she whispered, as David's hand fell from her slender shoulders.

As David frowned uneasily, she bit her lip. 'Oh, David, I hope not,' she groaned. 'Remember I'm supposed to be your maid.'

'Don't remind me,' he sighed tersely. 'I don't think he noticed, but you never know. Anyway,' he brightened, 'I was only giving you a hug, and while he would know me I'm sure he wouldn't recognise you. Last night you looked quite different, so I believe we can stop worrying. I don't think he would, but if he ever said anything to me I should simply tell him I was sharing a joke with my cousin.'

Gay frowned, still unwilling to discuss what had

happened the previous morning with anyone. Reluctantly she found herself agreeing with David that it was unlikely that Mr Ashley had recognised her, while feeling nervously sure that he had.

The remainder of the morning and afternoon passed uneventfully. After lunch the weather was so fine she took the children for a long walk. She put the baby in his pram and young David toddled beside her. When he grew tired she sat him on the end of the pram so that he could rest his short little legs. The fresh air made them all sleepy and after the children were in bed Gay made herself a pot of coffee, which she carried to the lounge.

Leaving the door slightly ajar, so she could hear if the children woke up, she stretched out luxuriously on the settee, propping her feet over the end of it with a sigh of relief. She felt rather ashamed that two young children were able to exhaust her. Most of her contemporaries would be out dining and dancing, not feeling too tired to move!

She was still sighing ruefully when the telephone rang, and as it was near, she merely moved a lazy hand and picked it up. It was her mother. Morris had apparently told her where Gay was and they talked for quite a while. Then Patricia Fenton asked her daughter what she was doing.

'I've got my feet up on Katrina's best settee,' Gay giggled. 'She's just had it covered and we scarcely dare look at it, let alone sit on it! She'd have a fit if she could see me now!'

'Well, just as long as you're there alone,' Patricia teased, 'I shan't worry too much.'

With that she said goodbye and rang off, leaving Gay to almost jump out of her skin as she glanced up to find Luke Ashley regarding her coldly. He was standing behind her, staring down at her, with the disapproving expression she was coming to recognise.

'Really, Mr Ashley!' Gay scrambled to her feet with a haste which she knew must make her look a lot guiltier than she felt. 'Why didn't you ring?' she demanded. 'You gave me an awful fright!'

'Perhaps it's what you need,' he replied grimly.

'How did you get in?' she stammered, trying not to notice the thick darkness of his hair, nor the decisiveness of his strongly featured face. He was a tall man, yet he moved with a kind of feline swiftness and looked as if he would be dangerous to cross.

'How did I get in?' he shrugged, his silvery eyes missing nothing as his glance flicked from the coffee pot to the heavy hair tumbled gloriously almost to her shoulders, 'The door was open and no one came when I rang, so I walked in.'

'That must have been young David,' she exclaimed. 'Doors are his thing, at the moment. He doesn't seem able to leave them alone. But I should have checked.'

'You would appear,' he drawled sarcastically, 'to have left undone those things which you ought to have done in order to concentrate on your own enjoyment.'

He had seen her feet on the end of the settee, just as he'd undoubtedly overheard her silly remarks about Katrina. Almost, she could see her crimes mounting up in his head! Coffee in the lounge while her employers were away. Using the telephone—probably to get in touch with a boy-friend. Not bothering to answer the doorbell, which she was certain must have rung at the same time as the telephone. It seemed his opinion of her couldn't get lower!

Gay forgot that, since he believed her to be the maid, his thoughts might reasonably be justified. Sullenly she retorted, 'I've been busy, very busy, all day.'

'So have millions of others,' he replied unsympathetically, 'but they don't all take advantage of their position.'

'All you need is a pulpit!' she snapped, again forgetting who she was supposed to be.

To her surprise, when she expected to be annihilated on the spot, he merely said shortly, 'I've never considered myself good enough for that, but I believe I know the difference between right and wrong.'

'While I don't?'

He said curtly, 'I'm beginning to doubt it.'

He was watching her closely and she felt a stab of impatience that she couldn't express herself more freely. It was unfortunate he had caught her as he had done, but what could she say? Without giving the game away her hands were tied. Fervently she wished she had never agreed to do as Katrina had asked. In retrospect it all seemed so silly and was rapidly getting out of hand. Complications were mounting at an alarming rate.

That Gay made no further attempt to defend herself appeared to anger him. 'If I employed a girl and found her making so free in my house, I'm afraid I wouldn't be lenient,' he told her sternly.

'What would you do to her, Mr Ashley?' Gay asked demurely, although she realised he might consider such a question impertinent.

If the set of his mouth was anything to go by, he did! 'I'd dismiss her,' he replied grimly.

'What a sense of power it must give you, even to know you're able to do that!' she commented dryly.

'Don't envy me,' he retorted harshly. 'Power is something that has to be worked damned hard for. It usually has to be paid for in blood and sweat.'

Gay blinked, noting, not for the first time, the hardness of his mouth and jaw, the stubborn strength of a deeply cleft chin. Would he be thirty-five or nearer forty? There was about him a kind of ruthless determination which defied age. If he was basically a rough diamond, as David had hinted, there was no sign of it in the cool sophistication of his face. All business deals would be a challenge. She suspected his rivals rarely stood a chance. Who would? she wondered, with a despair she didn't understand, before such calculating toughness, especially if he chose to turn on the charm at the same time.

Absorbed in her thoughts, she only slowly became

aware of his cynical amusement. 'You seem rather doubtful, Gay. Did you think success something which just happens overnight?'

'I'm not that naïve!' she exclaimed.

'I wonder?'

He was so dry she knew immediately he was thinking of David. Which had Gay's thoughts jumping apprehensively to Katrina. Here she was, allowing a mysterious resentment to drive her to antagonising Luke Ashley, while Katrina was relying on her to help David get a better job.

'Can I—I mean, will you have some coffee, Mr Ashley?' she faltered politely.

'Is that the best you can do?' he raised his brows.

'I don't understand, I'm afraid,' she frowned.

'I probably don't myself.' She saw his mouth tighten again. 'Forget it. I shouldn't have thought you were in any position to entertain here.'

She felt confused. 'I'm only offering coffee. As you're D—Mr Douglas's boss, they would expect me to.'

His eyes flickered as he noted how she almost used David's christian name, and she cursed his sharpness as much as her own continuing stupidity. He didn't mention it, though, but attacked on another subject. 'Have you had any proper training, Gay?'

'If you mean as a maid, no.' Colouring faintly, she wished he would stop showing interest, if that was what it was. 'Housework is mostly common sense, after all.'

'And the ability to avail yourself of the best while your employers are away?' he reproved coldly.

Gay gazed back at him, almost as coldly. Last night she had thought she had two different sides to her personality. Now she was sure Luke Ashley had too. Never would she have connected the grim, austere man in front of her with the one of yesterday morning, the man with flames in his eyes, who had kissed her so urgently. Or had she simply imagined it? Might it not have been her own emotions which she had seen reflected in the silvery sheen of his eyes?

'The children have been a handful today,' she forced herself to explain meekly. 'I was tired, and the Douglases don't mind if I use the lounge when they're away.'

'I see.'

Because of his derisive tones, her cheeks flamed and she found herself asking him sharply, 'Why did you call when you must have known they wouldn't be here? I can't believe it was just to spy on me.'

'No,' he agreed flatly, while the glint in his eye warned her she could go too far, 'it was not. It was the recipe for the duck casserole. My aunt forgot it last night and asked me to call and pick it up.'

'I forgot to write it down,' Gay reflected, wondering how she had managed to forget all about it. 'That is,' she stammered, 'Mrs Douglas did.'

'Do you know what was in it?'

'Yes,' she replied, feeling more foolish by the minute. 'If you can wait I'll find a pen and some paper.'

'There's no hurry,' he assured her, surprisingly. 'Perhaps I will have some coffee, after all.'

'I'm afraid it's cold.'

'Then make some more,' he commanded firmly.

In the kitchen Gay prayed he would go away, then hoped irrationally that he wouldn't be in too much of a hurry. What was the matter with her? she wondered, wishing she knew. Wasn't it essential to get him out of the house as quickly as possible, before she said something to irrevocably betray Katrina and David?

Returning to the lounge with fresh coffee, she tried to look anywhere but at Luke Ashley's dark, aloof face. She didn't need to look to know clearly that he wasn't a man who would appreciate being made a fool of. If they hadn't met as they had done, he might merely have been cynically amused by the little scheme which Katrina had innocently dreamt up to impress him. He might even have been a little flattered, but it was doubtful if he would ever have given the girl who had pretended to be the maid for the evening a second glance.

Yet mightn't she be allowing the effect of his fleeting interest to cloud her better judgment? All he seemed concerned with was her position in life and the way she apparently abused it. She might have caught his fancy, but only for a moment. He would never think seriously about a girl like herself. No, the hardness of his mouth was too calculating; it betrayed him as a man whose head ruled his heart. As he watched her, if he was doing anything, he was probably dissecting his emotions like a pathologist, with a cool curiosity as to why she had appealed even briefly to his senses. He might have found the answer as the cold satisfaction in his eyes increased. If he had been attracted it looked as if he had also found the perfect antidote.

Finding her gaze held by the mockery in his, she wasn't too surprised when he said suavely, 'I'm sorry if I upset you yesterday morning. I'm afraid I'd been up all night and been drinking.'

As her eyes went involuntarily over his hard, muscled body, Gay found it difficult to believe that losing a night's sleep would affect him in any way. As for drinking . . . hadn't he kissed her? She could have sworn he hadn't been within miles of anything alcoholic that morning. She didn't particularly dislike the smell of alcohol on a man's breath, but she had often used it as an excuse to avoid kissing someone. Her boy-friends didn't always believe it, of course, and frequently called her a cool little thing. Sometimes she often didn't understand herself why she felt no enthusiasm for kissing. If Luke Ashley had made her tremble and react differently, it must have been because of the unusual circumstances, rather than from any real emotion.

Now, perhaps understandably, he was seeking to excuse his brief lapse and it suited her to accept the explanation he had given. She actually felt a flicker of gratitude that he made it so easy.

'That's all right,' she murmured, lowering her thick lashes. 'We don't have to mention it again, Mr Ashley. In fact,' she shrugged, 'I'd almost forgotten.'

Luke Ashley regarded her silently for a moment or two, as though he wasn't sure if her response pleased him or not. If she hadn't been convinced he was a man who knew his own mind, she might have suspected him of being strangely uncertain. Well, he couldn't have it both ways, she felt like telling him, as his true purpose in coming here this evening seemed suddenly revealed. He had intended making sure she was harbouring no false hopes regarding himself. The recipe had merely been a formal excuse!

At last he said coolly, 'You're being very sensible about this, Gay.'

He didn't, she noticed, suggest she called him Luke. 'It often pays to be sensible,' she replied demurely, but so meaningly that she was secretly delighted at the faint tinge of colour which reddened his cheeks.

He raked a hand through his thick hair, his expression momentarily grim. 'Damn!' he muttered, staring at her with renewed coldness, clearly blaming her for his fleeting discomfiture. Then as she stirred uneasily beneath his cutting regard, the anger faded from his eyes and he enquired slowly:

'What made you go in for this kind of work, Gay?'

'I like housework,' she answered, not untruthfully.

This didn't appear to meet his approval. 'Aren't you trained for anything else?'

'I can type,' she admitted, 'but my shorthand's no good. Anyway,' she added deliberately, 'if I did train for a grand career, it's no guarantee of a job.'

'I could give you one,' he told her.

'In an office?'

'If you liked.'

'Oh, no, thanks,' she felt slightly apprehensive of his surprising offer and refused quickly. 'Er—my present employers couldn't do without me.'

She thought his glance went rather insultingly over her slender young body. 'Which one?' he drawled.

Gay coloured annoyingly. He didn't know she was referring to her job in London. Even so, she hated his contemptuous remarks. It made her clench her white teeth that she still had to be careful what she said, because of David.

While she restrained a tart reply with difficulty, he probed deeper. 'Wouldn't you rather be in London? It must be very quiet around here for a girl like you?'

Gay frowned. She didn't care for the contempt in his voice, the veiled insolence in his eyes. He was beginning to send shivers down her spine again. She could feel his dislike coming over in waves, with such intensity behind it that she wondered why he stayed.

'Just what sort of a girl do you think I am, Mr Ashley?' she challenged him fiercely, her eyes sparkling.

His glance went swiftly over her, making her regret asking, so intimate and thorough was his surveyal. She felt his eyes lingering on her face, then the gleaming mass of her silky hair before continuing over her high, pointed breasts to come to rest where her tight blue jeans clung too closely to her neatly rounded bottom. She felt as though his hands had followed his eyes and physically touched her.

Flushing scarlet, as she felt again the unaccountable tingling of yesterday, she was about to tell him rather wildly that she didn't really want to know what he thought of her, when she heard the baby crying upstairs.

'That will be Nigel!' she exclaimed, thanking heaven that something had intervened as she rushed from the room.

Nigel refused to be comforted, and after a few minutes Gay felt she dared stay upstairs no longer so she took him back to the lounge with her. Luke Ashley was still comfortably ensconced in an armchair. He had finished the coffee and taken the liberty, in her absence, to help himself to a large whisky.

He looked as if he needed it, she thought, confused. His mouth was grim and she felt his active dislike as he met the cool enquiry in her eyes. 'Don't worry,' he snapped, 'I'll certainly compensate your employer.'

Nigel cuddled close again and went to sleep. 'Does that mean,' she asked involuntarily, 'that you intend promoting him?'

Luke Ashley took another sip of his whisky. 'Not so he can keep two women. You can be sure of that at least, miss.'

Gay glared at him. 'What a man does with his money is surely his business. I only asked about his raise.'

'Did you?' his lips twisted. 'You don't believe it might depend on you?'

Feeling she could cheerfully have said something very unladylike, Gay clutched the baby closer and contented herself with a chilling glance. Surely he didn't seriously believe she was having some sort of an affair with David?

'You like children?' Luke Ashley ignored her anger. 'Do you ever think of having some of your own?'

'One day,' she said firmly, trying to stop her cheeks growing hot, 'I intend to.'

He stared at her and for some reason she found she couldn't look away.

'Just let me know . . .' he paused, his voice slightly thickening, 'if you should change your mind about the office.'

'How would I—be able to?' she muttered, half under her breath, scarcely realising what she was saying.

'I shall be looking in to see David again, Gay. You might be in London sooner than you think. In the city there are always better opportunities.'

Did he mean for David or herself? When he called again it wasn't likely she would be here. As he finished his drink and abruptly departed, Gay allowed herself a faint sigh of regret. Luke Ashley might be an arrogant dictator but, in other circumstances, she might have enjoyed knowing him better.

She didn't look up when he muttered a curt good-night, but just went on silently cuddling the baby.

CHAPTER THREE

GAY didn't see Luke Ashley again that weekend. He had forgotten the recipe he had called for, but when he rang and apologised she gave it to him over the phone. The children were demanding her attention and if she didn't do it this way it might get overlooked altogether. When he asked how she knew it so well, she said she had a very good memory.

When David arrived home on Sunday evening he was suffering from an extremely bad cold. It grew worse during the night and the doctor announced that he had influenza.

'Just my luck!' he groaned, as Gay popped her head around his door to say goodbye. 'But a couple of days in bed should see me all right.'

Blowing him an affectionate kiss, Gay said she hoped so. She had stayed as late as she dared, in order to give Katrina a hand with Nigel and young David when their father was ill, but she had to get back to London.

The weather had worsened again, and Gay shivered as the wind buffeted her as she left the bus to walk to the station. The almost gale force of it blew her hair in her eyes and tangled the strap of her shoulder bag around her suitcase.

On top of this, she was disconcerted to find Luke Ashley's powerful car pulling up beside her. Scarcely able to believe it could happen twice in the same place, she stared at him coldly.

He flung open the door on her side. 'Good afternoon,' he said, his eyes flicking from her face to the suitcase at her feet.

'Good afternoon,' she returned, coldly. 'Is this your beat?'

His mouth tightened, but otherwise he ignored her regrettable cheek. 'Where are you going?' he asked abruptly. 'You can't be due for another holiday yet?'

'You're parked on the double yellow,' she observed, as, with an impatient exclamation, he left the car to stand beside her.

'Then you'd better get in—or I'll make you responsible for my fine,' he snapped. 'You haven't answered my question. Where are you going with that suitcase?'

Gay grasped at a chance that seemed too good to miss. With two words she could tie everything up neatly, so prevent him embarrassing Katrina. Glancing away from him, she said quickly. 'I'm leaving.'

'Leaving?' his dark brows rose formidably.

'I got the sack, Mr Ashley.' She let her voice falter, impulsively deciding to make a good job of it.

'Why?' he wanted to know.

Immediately she regretted being so rash. There had to be a reason for getting the sack. Why hadn't she just said she'd taken a dislike to the town, or something impersonal like that? As she departed, Katrina, flustered and tired from the weekend and having to cope with a sick husband, had called after her, 'What'll I say if the Ashleys ask where you are?'

'They aren't likely to,' Gay had replied wearily, feeling she'd had enough of such foolish intrigue to last her the rest of her life. 'Oh, tell them I tried to set the house on fire!' she cried, as Katrina looked ready to burst into tears.

Gay hadn't reckoned on running into Luke Ashley again, and now she wished she had arranged something sensible with Katrina. Suddenly fed up, she longed to be home and tried hastily to remove herself from Luke Ashley's presence.

'I can't discuss the Douglases' private affairs,' she retorted deviously, turning away.

Luke grasped her arm, another thing she wished he

would stop doing. 'I'm not interested in the Douglases,' he drawled, 'I want to know about you.'

He wasn't interested in the Douglases! What did he mean by that? Not caring for the sound of it and still having their welfare at heart, Gay thought twice about being really rude.

'I'm sorry,' she murmured. 'Now, if you'd please excuse me . . .'

His grip on her arm tightened, showing he wasn't willing to. 'Right,' he agreed tersely, 'no more questions, but there's surely nothing to prevent you from telling me where you're going. Or don't you know?'

'Of course I do!' she snapped, wishing he wasn't so tall and overpowering, 'I'm going to catch my connection to London—when you decide to let go of me!'

Again he ignored her request. 'So you can't resist the lure of the big city?' he observed cynically. 'Have you ever spent much time there?'

'I live there—usually.' She wondered why he need look so grimly calculating. Suddenly nervous, beyond anything she had ever known, she tried to free herself by wrenching at his hand with her own.

The sensation was immediate. As she touched his bare fingers it shot through her like a flash of lightning. Immediately she withdrew, her breath catching wildly in the sudden rawness of her throat.

'Look,' he suggested tightly, his own breath roughening slightly, 'I'm on my way to London. Come with me?' The apprehension she felt must have been reflected in her widening eyes, for he added sardonically, 'I'm only offering a lift.'

'Why?'

For a moment he looked grim, as though he wasn't quite sure himself. 'Do we have to find reasons for everything?' he muttered curtly. 'Let's just say you'll be someone to talk to.'

Gay, still doubtful, groped futilely for a convincing excuse, but before she could think of anything she found herself thrust inside his car with her luggage in the back. 'We can't stand arguing all day!' he snapped.

As he drove off swiftly, Gay muttered angrily, 'Do you always use such high-handed methods to get your own way?'

'With dithering females it's the only way,' Luke said crisply, as they left the last houses behind them.

Simmering almost to boiling point, Gay found it difficult to control her temper. Then she remembered something. There was surely no need to restrain herself any longer. Wasn't she supposed to have got the sack?

But before she could launch into an attack, he took the wind from her sails by asking, with a hint of confusing anxiety, 'What do you propose doing now?'

Realising she must still be cautious, she replied briefly, 'Find another job.'

'I could help.' Surprisingly, he sounded almost as cautious as she did. 'What about something secretarial?'

'I thought we'd disposed of that on Saturday?' she reminded him. 'Anyway, I'd probably suffocate in an office.'

'Not in one of mine, you wouldn't.'

He hinted at super, air-conditioned luxury and she shot him a cold glance. 'I'm not properly trained. Were you thinking of using me as an ornament, Mr Ashley?'

His brows quirked. 'You'd make a very decorative one. I've known a few redheads, but never one with your beautifully soft colouring. You might have sat for one of those wonderful old paintings. Perhaps a Titian?'

Because his reply seemed to affect her strangely, she uttered sharply, 'Well, I don't intend decorating any residence of yours, Mr Ashley!'

'I wouldn't want a girl like you merely to stare at,' he countered.

Before she could regain her breath, he went on to ask coolly, 'Whereabouts in London do you live? I presume you do have a proper address?'

Gay almost told him, but changed her mind. 'I usually

stay with people I know, or my—er—brother.'

'Is anyone expecting you?'

'Not really,' she replied, without thinking, suddenly a trifle desolate.

'So you can't be in any particular hurry to get back.' He glanced at her swiftly, his brows raised.

'No,' she agreed slowly, again realising how her hands were tied. How could she tell him about the boutique, when he believed she had been working for Katrina? 'I don't want to be late, though,' she added more hurriedly. 'Why do you ask?'

'I thought we might go on somewhere and have a cup of tea together.'

'You said you were going straight to London?' she said suspiciously.

'Don't look so nervous, Gay,' he rejoined cynically, 'I have no intention of making a pass at you. I'd like to know you a little better before doing that.'

'You didn't hesitate on Friday morning!' she retorted, then wished angrily that she had held her tongue.

'A momentary insanity,' he replied curtly, 'as I believe I explained. Don't worry, it won't happen again.'

'Can I trust you?' she asked acidly, annoyed with herself for not appreciating such a promise.

'I'm not sure,' he admitted, 'that I can trust myself, but we can both try!'

As he apparently took her consent for granted and they drove deeper into the country, Gay tried to relax. There was only Morris in London and he mightn't be so very pleased to see her. An hour or two would make no difference, she supposed.

'Do you commute?' she asked, as the silence between them lengthened.

'I have been, for my aunt's sake,' said Luke.

'You're very fond of her?'

'Yes,' he agreed.

Gay felt there was a depth to his voice when he spoke of his aunt which was missing when he mentioned other people. 'You appreciate your aunt because she's elderly and never argues with you,' she said dryly, remembering how Miss Ashley had seemed to agree with her nephew about everything.

'I appreciate Dora because she's nice, and always has been,' he assured Gay coldly, sensing criticism. Then he confused her completely by adding, 'The trouble is she's never been used to anything but a very humble cottage, and I don't think she's capable of adapting.'

'You'll have to give her time,' Gay advised, trying to recall what she could of the neat little woman he had brought to dinner. She hadn't been the paragon Katrina had feared—she was pleasant, quiet and ordinary. And, because of this, Gay suspected Luke Ashley could be right. His aunt certainly didn't seem cut out for high society—at least not the circles he liked to move in!

'I don't think time's going to make all that much difference,' he frowned. 'I have a feeling she's already given up.'

Gay glanced at him sharply. 'Doesn't she like being a lady? I mean, the sort you're trying to turn her into?'

'I'm not trying to turn her into anything,' he retorted, quite aware of Gay's sarcasm. 'It's simply a matter of moving up in the world, which I find few people can do successfully. The house was my aunt's idea, but she still clings to her old way of life. This morning she was talking of going back to her cottage. So now what do I do?'

'You'll just have to make sure you don't make the same mistake twice,' Gay taunted. 'You mightn't so easily get rid of a wife who didn't come up to scratch.'

'I'd get rid of her soon enough if she talked as you do,' he said menacingly. 'But don't worry, my wife will certainly fit in.'

'Will she be chosen for her pedigree or because you love her?' Gay laughed scornfully.

'The former,' he snapped.

Her indifferent taunting might have been an irritating fly, for all the notice he took of it. She stared at him in amazement, feeling curiously hollow. 'But . . . what about affection—love?' she faltered.

'I don't believe in it. Attraction, yes,' he allowed without expression, 'but that's something which can be worked out of the system quite easily, with a little common sense.'

His supreme confidence in his ability to control his emotions left Gay gasping incredulously. One day, she hoped fervently, some woman might have him crying for mercy, drowning in his own so-called common sense. She was dubious, though, sensing his implacable hardness, if that day would ever come.

An odd fascination gripping her, she dared another question. 'If you aren't waiting for love then why haven't you already chosen a wife? You're surely old enough?'

'Thirty-six,' he answered coolly, his hands on the steering wheel completely relaxed, as if he considered his age of no consequence. Idly he shrugged his broad shoulders. 'I've been busy, perhaps that's why I've never married. I expect David Douglas has told you, for I believe it's no secret, that I started at the bottom. It's taken a hell of a lot of doing, getting where I am today, but I have no regrets. Now, however, I feel I could take time to put my domestic life in order.'

Softly, Gay exploded, 'I've never heard anything quite so cold-blooded!'

'Oh, my blood's far from cold,' he quipped, his hard, sensuous mouth curving in a way that quickened Gay's pulses irrationally. 'Well bred women often have ice in their veins, I've found, but as long as my future wife knows how to conduct herself, I'll not complain.'

'How magnanimous of you,' she said bleakly.

'Never mind,' he replied, 'my marriage won't concern you.'

She considered his marriage with a kind of morbid curiosity. 'Have you anyone in mind?'

'One or two,' he watched Gay's face with a kind of

brooding intensity, 'I haven't come to any definite decision.'

As his eyes returned to the road, Gay released a deep breath. 'I suppose you take it for granted that, whoever the fortunate lady is, she'll accept you?'

He smiled cynically. 'She might resist me, but not my money.'

Gay fell silent, feeling suddenly depressed. 'Why are you telling me all this?' she asked at last.

Luke looked faintly surprised, as if it had only just occurred to him how much of himself he was revealing. 'I'm not sure. I know I find you easy to talk to, despite our differences. It's more probably because you're a stranger, whom I won't be seeing again once we reach London. What would be the point?' he muttered, as if to himself.

At least he was honest, Gay thought wryly. And she certainly didn't want to see him again! So why did her sinking spirits not lift?

'Have you had any lunch?' His eyes, which for unknown reasons, kept returning to her pale face, held a hint of reluctant anxiety. 'I suggested tea, but perhaps we should make it something more substantial?'

'I'm not hungry, but I shouldn't mind a sandwich,' she admitted, averting her eyes quickly from his hard, handsome features. She had been so busy with the children, she hadn't had time for much lunch.

They had sandwiches and scones and a huge pot of tea in a pleasant country hotel. Luke Ashley didn't eat much. Sitting back in his chair, he watched Gay appraisingly, a frown frequently marking his broad forehead. While she was drinking her second cup of tea and unashamedly enjoying a huge piece of chocolate gateau, he excused himself to make a phone call.

'I won't be long,' he said, and Gay smiled at him.

As the double oak doors of the tea lounge closed behind his tall, decisive figure, she wondered why he had looked so odd when she had smiled at him. He hadn't seen her smile before; perhaps that was why he had been so startled. For the past hour she had been very conscious of his narrow regard, which had varied from being quite pleasant to coldly calculating. Most of the time she had also been aware of her own mounting interest, but she doubted if Luke Ashley shared her accelerated heartbeat, or suffered from the same mysterious weak feeling of longing.

Whatever happened, she told herself firmly, she mustn't let this man get under her skin. He was hard and though he confessed to having risen from the bottom, he had obviously developed into a first-rate snob—just the type she despised. He would be as coldly calculating about his marriage as he would about his other relationships. Instinctively she felt, when the mood took him, he would be passionate enough to please any woman. Yet who wanted a man who controlled his emotions like a tap, running them hot or cold, as he chose?

Fiercely glad now that she wouldn't be seeing him again, she waited morosely for his return. He was away about ten minutes and she tried to still her inward tremors as he walked back towards her.

His grimness dismayed her. For all she disliked him, she hoped he hadn't had bad news. Pausing beside her, he said curtly, 'If you're quite ready we'll go.'

Obediently, without bothering to reply, Gay gathered up her coat and bag. Abruptly he turned away and she followed him from the hotel.

The sun had disappeared behind a cloud, which looked no darker than Luke Ashley's face. What now? she sighed, realising she hadn't mistaken his change of mood. It seemed incredible that Luke Ashley, of all people, was giving her a lift to London, but then a lot of things that had happened in the past three days seemed scarcely believable. And, from the expression on Mr Ashley's face, there was more to come!

He drove off without speaking, leaving Gay feeling almost reprieved. Yet she couldn't help glancing at him nervously, apprehensive of the smouldering anger in his eyes. A few miles along the highway he turned off on to a quieter country road. Here there was very little traffic and eventually he drew up on a deserted layby.

Gay turned to him in surprise. 'Where are we? Why are we stopping?' she enquired anxiously.

'We aren't far from London, and we've stopped because I want a word with you,' he replied.

Puzzled, Gay waited for him to continue. His jaw was taut, he looked grim, but then she had rarely seen him looking otherwise. Not in her company!

He swivelled around on her swiftly, disregarding the underlying innocence in her face. He didn't hesitate. His was the pounce of the assailant, the slashing attack of an enemy, determined to vanquish with one blow.

'I rang the Douglases while you were finishing your tea,' he informed her, his silvery gaze resembling ice. 'Mrs Douglas told me she'd dismissed you for indiscreet behaviour. She hinted that it had something to do with her husband.'

'She—she can't have done!' Gay stammered.

'Isn't it true?' he asked silkily. 'Before you deny it, remember I caught you twice.'

'Tw—twice?' Gay heard herself continuing to stammer; she also felt herself going hot and then cold. Knowing nicely the two occasions Luke Ashley referred to, she searched desperately for a means of establishing her innocence, without making Katrina out to be a liar.

'Twice,' he repeated cuttingly.

Gay's cheeks burned. 'Oh, believe what you like!' she cried indignantly. 'Mrs Douglas imagines things—well, sometimes . . .'

'So you aren't having an affair with her husband?'

'No!' she denied hotly.

'Then why did you leave? I'd like the truth this time, if you please. I won't be put off again.'

Who did he think he was? 'I'd rather not say,' she muttered, half desperately, thinking he might be more than she could handle. Not for the first time did she feel completely frustrated by a situation she found impossible to explain.

'You were good with the children,' he began, with the same cool thoroughness he might have used in the boardroom, 'a good cook,' as Gay blinked, he enlightened her, 'I happen to know who cooked Friday's dinner. Your work couldn't be faulted, so it has to be something else. You realise I saw you with David Douglas on Saturday?'

'He—he was only being friendly.'

'Really?' Luke Ashley's expression was ironic. 'I've never been quite so warmly disposed towards any maid of mine.'

'It—it wasn't what you think!' she reiterated wildly.

His eyes glinted dangerously. 'Do you mean to tell me that Mrs Douglas imagined everything? That her husband has ever actually had you in his arms? Never kissed you?'

'Of course not!' Gay glared. 'Not the way you mean, anyway,' she faltered rashly.

The rage in Luke Ashley's eyes deepened. 'Perhaps you would care to be more explicit?'

'Oh, damn!' she exclaimed aloud, using language she rarely indulged in. But why didn't he shut up! How could she explain, without giving everything away, that all her life David had treated her with a brotherly affection which very occasionally included a hug or a light peck on the cheek? 'You'd like to tie me in knots, wouldn't you?' she accused Luke Ashley.

'Yes,' he agreed tightly, 'for the sole purpose of extracting the truth.'

'Listen,' she leaned nearer, gripping his arm in an unconscious attempt to make him understand, 'I left the Douglases because I wanted to. Nobody has done anything bad enough for you to get hot and bothered about. Men do glance at other girls and their wives sometimes get suspicious, but believe me, imagination often plays the greater part. Anyway, what business is it of yours, Mr Ashley? Why should it bother you to this extent?'

'You could be right,' he snapped impatiently. 'I'm damned if I know. At least we appear to have established that it wasn't Douglas's fault. Not entirely, anyway. It was more the fault of a foolish young girl, out for fun.'

'Thank you for nothing!' Gay retorted tartly, trying to cover a strange hurt. She knew she should only be feeling relieved that Katrina and David had apparently been exonerated and she couldn't account for her reluctance to let Luke Ashley believe her the guilty party. What, after all, did it matter?

'Girls do look for a little fun,' she agreed, thinking she might well be hanged for a pound as a penny!

'My God!' Luke Ashley caught hold of her shouders in an angry grasp, his fingers biting through the thickness of her coat. 'You deserve a good fright, and there might be only one way of dealing with a girl like you—to give you one!'

Letting go of his arm with a gasp, having quite forgotten she was holding it, Gay tried to break free. His eyes were angry but betrayed only a desire to reprimand by means of physical violence, in the form perhaps of a good shake. Why then were they both inexplicably overwhelmed by the force of an attraction which had already drawn them together several times?

Suddenly the hands on Gay's shoulders were slipping down her back, while the space between them closed. His breath was on her face, then her mouth, while one of his hands returned swiftly to slide through her silky hair, so she couldn't escape him.

Their eyes met and clashed with suffocating intensity and a pulse beat wildly in Gay's throat. She seemed at that moment to have no weapons to fight him with and trembled involuntarily. The man's power was frightening; she realised she should have known better than to tangle with it. 'Please let me go,' she whispered.

Silently he shook his head. 'Not yet,' he said thickly.

The tension between them had her heart beating dizzily and her whole being drowning in new sensations. Their eyes fused until her heavy lashes fell helplessly. Then they were closer, blending together, Luke's mouth against her own in a kiss like none other. Wordlessly they clung together, his hands holding her prisoner. She had never experienced such an emotional invasion. In all her young life she had never known passion in any form; now she was feeling for the first time the onslaught of a man's sexual power and responding blindly. Under his expert guidance she was becoming wholly alive.

Her arms slid around his neck and she clung to him, suddenly uncaring of what he was doing to her. She felt hypnotised, her head spinning, as a reckless feeling of pleasure swamped her ability to think. She knew he was just getting rid of his anger, but the immediate awakening of her own needs made her deaf to the small voice of caution.

Then suddenly, with a cruel abruptness, he pulled himself away. Even so, she was so dazed she didn't feel the full weight of his rejection until he spoke.

Drawing firmly back into his own seat, he said curtly, 'The sooner I get you to London and out of my life the better.'

He didn't apologise or say anything pleasant. Gay supposed she couldn't expect him to. What had happened hadn't been intentional. She was certain he hadn't set out to kiss her and she must be as much to blame as he was. All the same, she felt terribly shaken and her stomach was behaving in the most peculiar way.

His face was pale, she noticed, and he fumbled slightly with the gears as he started the car, but otherwise he appeared as distant as ever. Gay was surprised to realise she was growing beautifully numb herself. It seemed to prove that the blinding sensations which had swept through her as Luke Ashley had held her in his arms had merely been transitory.

He didn't speak again until they reached London, and then it was only to ask whereabouts she lived.

Glancing at him quickly, she gave Morris's address. Morris's flat was near the river. The area had been mostly slums when Morris had moved in but was rapidly becoming fashionable. Because of this he talked of moving on, but hadn't done so yet. He liked the river and its moods. He said it soothed him.

It was quite obvious that Luke Ashley was far from impressed as he followed Gay's directions. Yet when he drew up and she scrambled out, he picked up her suitcase and followed.

'Lead the way,' he ordered tersely, glancing, frowning, at the shadowed alleyways, the dark, cobbled streets. The waters of the Thames lapped eerily against the embankment and she shivered.

'It's not as bad as it seems,' Gay felt driven to protest, because of his expression.

'Really?'

'I can manage!' The irony in his voice angered her and her hand went out to retrieve her case.

'I said, lead the way!' he repeated.

With a little shrug she gave in, already sensing the futility of arguing with him. 'If you must,' she sniffed.

'What the hell am I supposed to do?' he exclaimed. 'Leave you to the mercy of every thug that comes along? I'd advise you to find another living-in job as soon as possible.'

'I've never even had a fright,' she replied, ignoring what he said about a job.

'There's a first time for everything,' he taunted, and she trembled at something indefinable in his voice as he followed her up the dark, twisting stairs.

'Your brother must be mad, letting you run risks like this,' he snapped, as they neared the top.

'We can't all live in penthouses,' she snapped back.

Taking the key from her bag outside the flat, she

fumbled with the lock, while he waited with reprehensible impatience. As the door swung open and she turned with a hurried word of thanks for her suitcase, Julie appeared with Morris close behind her.

Gay felt her cheeks flame as she saw Julie was again wearing her almost transparent negligee. Julie stared at her glumly, making Gay feel far from welcome. Luke Ashley, with a cynical nod, merely turned and left them. He didn't even bother to say goodbye.

Morris's eyes were half on his sister, half on Luke Ashley's retreating figure. 'I wasn't expecting you, Gay,' he said sharply, putting an arm around Julie.

What he meant was, he hadn't expected her as late as this. Usually she returned earlier from the Douglases' and he met her at the station. He had told her, when she was coming home, always to ring. It wasn't his fault she had forgotten.

'I'm sorry, Morris,' her eyes went uncertainly to Julie. 'I can easily go elsewhere.'

'No, it doesn't matter,' he groaned. 'We'll arrange something.'

Behind her, Gay heard the footsteps, which had paused, continue down the stairs. Had Luke lingered to hear Morris's answer, or to catch a glimpse of how the other half lived? Through the shabby door she caught sight of an even worse than usual untidiness and wondered why it had never bothered her all that much until now.

'Who was that super-looking man?' Julie wanted to know, as soon as the door closed. 'Was he with you?'

Gay nodded. 'He's a neighbour of the friends I've been staying with. He gave me a lift.' She didn't say who he was and Julie didn't ask for more specific details, being too much in love with Morris to be able to concentrate very long on anyone else.

Julie was nice, but Gay had often considered her foolish for being so infatuated with Morris, who clearly put his career first. Now Gay wasn't so sure. Recalling how she had felt in Luke Ashley's arms, she was beginning to realise just how easy it might be to become fully committed to one special man.

She still hadn't managed to get Luke completely out of her mind by the time Morris left to take Julie home. With a sigh she undressed and went to bed, taking a book she had been meaning to read for ages. What was the use of dreaming, she chided herself, about a man who had never once asked her to use his christian name, and who was such a snob that when it came to marriage, apparently only a duchess would do!

The next morning she rose at six and, to Morris's disgust, began tidying the flat.

'There's nothing wrong with it as it is!' He thrust an enraged head around his bedroom door as the Hoover woke him up.

'It's filthy!' Gay yelled, above the noise of the machine. 'I should have done something about it before now.'

'I like it,' Morris snarled, having missed Julie through the night more than he cared to admit. 'What's got into you, Gay?'

'I don't know . . .' Stopping the machine, she stared at her brother helplessly.

'You're always at me about it, Gay, but it's never actually bothered you before. You know I can't work in tidy surroundings, so why the sudden panic?' He ran a thoughtful hand around the roughness of his chin. 'It can't have anything to do with that superior-looking character who brought you home last night?'

'Oh, don't be silly!' Gay pressed the Hoover into action again, deafening his mocking reply.

A little later, when she finished, she found him in the kitchen, waving a hot cup of tea. 'Come on,' he grinned, 'you must be parched after all that. And you can tell me all about it.'

Of course she didn't tell Morris anything, for there was nothing really logical to tell, and she didn't expect to see Luke again, unless, perhaps, in a newspaper. It was on the following Saturday morning, when because she was somehow feeling pretty low, she treated herself to a glass of fizzy orange and a sticky, calorie-mad cream bun in one of London's most famous stores, that she spotted him having coffee with a slinky, dark-haired lady.

Hurriedly Gay looked the other way, startled to find her hands shaking. Unless she was mistaken, the girl whom he was with was a customer of the boutique and very high society indeed. Yes, it was Lily Dalmonte, right enough. As some people rose from the table between them, Gay had a better view. Well, Luke Ashley was certainly aiming high enough there, but from the simpering, adoring expression on Lily's face, it looked as if she might be more than willing to take him on.

Blankly, Gay stared down at her fizzy drink, wondering why it should suddenly taste so bitter. Darting another quick glance at the back of Luke's dark head, she saw he was looking as hard and fit as ever. He was handsome enough to be attracting plenty of surreptitious glances from the women around him, but he appeared to be concentrating solely on his companion. He even placed a hand over Lily Dalmonte's on the table, leaving Gay feeling slightly sick.

So Luke must have been serious when he talked of marrying well. Gay shivered, unable to account for the coldness which suddenly invaded her. Reluctantly she supposed it had something to do with the way she was feeling. Ever since she had met Luke she had found it difficult to stop thinking of him. With a sigh she rose, gathering up her belongings, her face oddly strained. She might have known her vague hopes that he might get in touch with her again would come to nothing.

CHAPTER FOUR

Two days later, though, he did get in touch with her again. Morris had gone abroad on a commission from one of the leading fashion houses. He had taken Julie and two other models, and Gay found herself wishing she could have gone with them. Some sunshine and a change of scene might have cheered her up and stopped her from dreaming of the unobtainable!

She had expected it to be either Morris or her mother on the telephone when it rang. That it was Luke startled her.

'Gay? Luke Ashley here.'

'Oh,' she stammered, after a breathless silence, 'hello, Mr Ashley.'

'Are you doing anything this evening?' he asked abruptly.

'Not really . . .'

'Have dinner with me, then. I'll pick you up in an hour. Right?'

'If you like.'

Gay dropped the receiver as if it was red hot, then sat staring at it. What on earth had made her agree to go out with him so quickly? Had she no pride? What on earth did he want to see her about, anyway? Another lecture on how not to behave with married men? He had been abrupt to the point of rudeness, as though it mattered little to him whether or not she accepted his invitation. She had the disquieting impression that he even despised himself somewhat for issuing it in the first place.

She was ready when he called for her. Having spent the greater part of the hour he had allocated wondering what to wear, she didn't think she was going to make it. She kept telling herself she was crazy to bother, but that didn't prevent her making feverish preparations.

Guessing he would probably take a girl like herself to a quiet spot where there would be no danger of running into any of his snooty friends, she settled for something plain and simple. The dress she wore had been a sale reduction from the boutique—Morris had declared it a mistake, with no lack of brotherly candour. But that it didn't particularly suit her seemed to make it all the more appropriate for this evening as she didn't want Luke Ashley to think she had set out to impress him.

Long before the doorbell rang, she was taut with nervous tension. She realised she had had a frightening suspicion he wouldn't turn up and had been bracing herself against such an eventuality. Having always hated pretension of any kind, she couldn't understand why she gazed at the door a full minute before making any move to answer it.

Luke was about to ring again when she appeared. 'You took your time,' he muttered, but seemed more preoccupied with the way she looked than her reply. His eyes went closely over her, his examination so thorough she shivered.

'Am I the right girl?' she queried, trying to hide her own reactions with sarcasm.

'I'm sorry,' he actually apologised. 'Good evening, Gay.'

'Good evening, Mr Ashley.' Drawing a tremulous little breath, she deliberately emphasised the Mr.

'You'd better call me Luke.' His eyes were still exploring. He sounded almost absentminded.

'Not if you're not sure,' she replied coolly.

'Oh, for heaven's sake!' he snapped. Then, more evenly, 'Aren't you going to ask me in?'

'I'd rather not.' As his brows rose, she knew, for some indefinable reason, she couldn't trust herself alone with him in the flat. Because she couldn't tell him this she added, she hoped discouragingly, 'We aren't very smart, I'm afraid.'

'You forget,' he retorted, as they went down the stairs, 'I used to live in a similar place myself once. Somehow I managed to keep it tidy, though.'

Gay coloured faintly at the hint of criticism. 'I've been trying to do something about it.' She didn't mention Morris's insistence that too much tidiness stifled his creativeness. But, as they settled in the car and Luke's brows quirked derisively, she was provoked to add, 'My brother is away just now, but it's difficult to keep the flat decent when he's at home.'

In the act of switching the ignition, Luke paused abruptly. 'Do you mean to say you're living there alone?'

'Why not?' She stuck her feet out straight in front of her, staring at them. 'Who's to harm me?'

'If you say that once again, I will!' he spoke between his teeth.

'Don't worry,' she managed to look faintly amused, 'I'll survive.'

'Alley cats usually do,' he rejoined curtly, 'but they need to be tough. Tougher, I think, than you are.'

'Perhaps,' she agreed carelessly, as with a grim sigh he swung the large, luxurious car into the road. Yet there was nothing careless in the glance she bestowed on him, as he concentrated on the rather tortuous detour to the main thoroughfare. Gay was aware of a feverish need inside her to refresh her memory intimately with every detail of that strong profile.

Disconcerted by the intensity of her gaze and apprehensive that he might sense it, she attempted to break his disapproving silence. 'Why did you ask me out tonight when it seems your opinion of me couldn't get lower?'

She suspected he had had a poor opinion of her all along, yet felt oddly hurt when he didn't deny it. Tonight his broad shoulders merely lifted indifferently. 'I'm not sure why I rang you. I believe I was curious to a certain extent.'

'Curious?'

'As to how you were getting on. Whether or not you'd managed to get another job. And the place where you live worries me, though don't ask me to be more explicit, for I've really no idea why it should.'

Considering how she couldn't find a logical reason, either, for some of the things which troubled her about him, Gay thought it might be wiser to drop the subject. 'I have a part-time job in a small shop,' she told him reluctantly.

This didn't appear to impress. 'Why didn't you try for a living-in job, as I advised? Or were you frightened you might get involved with another husband?'

'That's a horrid thing to say!' Gay exclaimed angrily.

'The truth can't always be wrapped up so it doesn't hurt,' he rejoined sharply.

'I suppose not,' she sighed impatiently, 'but you ought to make sure of your facts before you start slamming them at people.'

'I'm never far wrong,' he replied dryly.

Mutinously, Gay returned to staring at her feet. Why should he be so concerned for her morals? That he imagined she had been having an affair with David no longer afforded her any amusement. She had been in touch with Katrina. David was being promoted—but abroad. He had been promised if he did a year overseas, he could come back to London permanently.

They were to go very soon. Gay didn't think she would see them before they left. Katrina had been breathlessly excited when Gay spoke to her. Everything was being done for them, even their packing. David was still not sure what had hit him. He and his family would be on the boat almost before he had had time to recover from the 'flu. They could have flown, but Mr Ashley had said a sea voyage would do him more good.

Katrina hadn't mentioned her conversation with Luke

regarding Gay's sudden departure, and somehow Gay hadn't the heart to tackle her about it. Better to forget it, she had decided, wishing Katrina bon voyage.

After a few minutes Luke turned his dark head to glance at her. 'You've gone very quiet.'

'I've been thinking,' she replied innocently, 'don't you need a cook, Mr Ashley? You enjoyed my cooking, and good cooks are hard to come by.'

'No, I do not!' His eyes went cold, as if he found even the thought of having her in his house disturbing. 'I like to be able to relax when I get home at night.'

'I'm a very quiet worker,' she assured him solemnly, 'I don't bang my pans about, and you'd be able to keep an eye on me—without having to take me out.'

'Oh, for God's sake shut up!' he exclaimed. 'Right now I don't have a sense of humour.'

The opportunity seemed suddenly too good to miss. 'I could always ask the Douglases to take me back.'

'Not possible,' he replied abruptly. 'They're going overseas and I've already arranged their domestic help.'

'Good gracious!' Gay tried to make her surprise sound naïvely genuine. 'Whatever for?'

'Damn it, girl,' he muttered tersely, 'do you always demand reasons for everything? Your late employer needs experience, but not the kind you seemed bent on supplying!'

Gay didn't bother to reply but lapsed into silence again as they drove out of the city. The big car ate up the miles and the twilight deepened into darkness, but somehow the atmosphere between them, despite their differences, wasn't strained. Again Gay was conscious of the underlying tug between them of something basic. If Luke's glance sought hers for a second, her own responded, as though drawn by a magnet. And when his hand accidentally brushed hers, when he changed gear, she had the curious sensation of being flicked all over by lightning. Remembering Lily Dalmonte, she stirred uneasily. After this evening she would be a fool to see

Luke again, even if he asked her.

The riverside restaurant he took her to was quiet, but there was music and dancing. As she had suspected it might be, the place he chose was well off the beaten track. There wouldn't be much risk of running into anyone either of them knew.

'Your fine friends would never find you here,' Gay taunted as they sat down. The table Luke had asked for was well tucked out of sight, but she dismissed the notion that he had wanted it because it was small and intimate. She preferred to believe it was because he wanted to run as little risk as possible of being seen with her.

'We both have friends,' he reminded her, 'who might raise their eyebrows if they saw us together.'

How true, she mused, trying to imagine her mother's face and stifling a giggle. 'As usual, you're right,' she acknowledged more soberly.

They ate well, but while Luke seemed disinclined to hurry, he didn't once ask her to dance. Gay had a feeling he would have liked to but was wary about having her in his arms. Twice, as he glanced towards the small orchestra, she felt he was about to suggest it, only to see his mouth tighten while, almost imperceptibly, he shook his head.

What was there about her that made him so reticent where she was concerned? Gay wondered, feeling curiously disappointed. He had asked her out yet seemed determined to keep her at arm's length. Scornful of a fast beating pulse, she told herself firmly it was just as well.

After a while, as the tension inside her eased a little, she was surprised to find him quite easy to talk to. She was surprised, too, as the evening wore on, at the number of things they discussed and agreed upon. As long as they kept off anything too personal. From this they both shied with a caution they both seemed to share.

Over coffee he returned to the matter of her employment. 'I'd feel happier if you were living with a family. Somewhere where you'd be safer when your brother goes off with his girl-friends.'

'He's working,' she defended Morris, 'not enjoying himself.'

'He hadn't work in mind the other night,' Luke said cynically.

'That was only Julie,' Gay sighed. 'It's surely no crime for a man of his age to have a girl-friend? What about yourself? I saw you with a woman on Saturday and you looked as if you thought her pretty special.'

If Gay had hoped to divert his attention from Morris before he delved any deeper, she appeared to have succeeded. 'Where did you see me?' he asked sharply.

'I was in the West End. You were having coffee.'

He was silent for a moment, then said, 'Miss Dalmonte had been shopping, and I'd arranged to pick her up.'

'How nice—for Miss Dalmonte,' Gay smiled, while her heart felt heavy. She was aware of Luke's critical appraisal. Was he comparing her with the illustrious Lily Dalmonte and finding her wanting? 'Your friend certainly has class!' she added deliberately.

Luke's eyes narrowed unpleasantly. 'Must you talk like that?'

'Are you going to marry her?' Gay persisted.

'I might,' he answered tersely, a slight frown creasing his handsome forehead.

Gay's throat hurt, but she forced herself to say lightly, 'You could do worse.'

He replied with harsh certainty, 'I could scarcely do better.'

'So,' Gay stared at his hand, lying clenched on the table, 'what's the problem?'

'No problem,' he snapped. 'I simply like to take my time.'

'Oh, all right!' Gay lifted defiant eyes to meet his. 'I'll shut up—I can take a hint. You can let me know when your engagement's announced and I'll send you one of those nice wish you well cards.'

'Gay,' he said curtly, 'will you kindly shut up!'

Gay blinked. His voice warned her not to pile it on too thickly. Luke Ashley was no fool. 'I'm sorry,' she said meekly, lowering her eyes. 'It's none of my business, I know.'

'No, it's not,' he agreed, his own eyes glinting. Rising to his feet, he said firmly, 'I think I'd better take you home.'

Gay was sleeping when they reached the flat. Her head had somehow slipped to his shoulder and she sat up with a jerk when the car stopped. A strand of her soft red hair was entangled around one of his buttons and he laughed gently as he freed it.

'You've got beautiful hair,' he teased softly. 'At the moment your cheeks are the same colour.'

'I fell asleep,' she stammered foolishly, pulling away from him.

'Yes,' he was watching her closely, 'I had to hold you to prevent you tumbling over, but you were nice and soft and warm.'

Flushed with confusion, she scrambled from the car. 'Goodnight, Luke.'

He was beside her on the pavement, as quickly as he had been the first time he had brought her home. With a raised hand he silenced her protests, escorting her sternly up the creaking wooden stairs.

'Let me come in for five minutes?' he asked, as she opened the door.

Somehow she couldn't resist the unconscious urgency in his voice. The blood pounded in her head as she nodded.

Inside he made no attempt to deviate but drew her slowly towards him. 'I don't want coffee or a drink, or even to stay long. I just want to say goodnight properly, without the risk of interruption.'

'Why?' she whispered huskily.

'Answer not known,' he replied, with a kind of cool mockery which might have been directed at himself as much as her.

With a quick movement he pulled her closer, so near she could see the strange excitement in his eyes. Silently he held her to him, one arm encircling her shoulders, and an electric shock raced through her body as she was crushed against his hard chest and his free hand tilted up her chin. His lips met hers lightly at first, but her trembling response brought an increasing passion to his kiss. Slowly, as her lips parted under his, he began exploring her mouth more deeply. Their arms tightened, their bodies fused and a slow fire began spreading along Gay's limbs.

She was so terrified of this alien sensation that she dragged herself away from him. 'Please go now,' she cried. 'I don't want you here.'

'Yes,' his breathing was harsh while his eyes were dark and smouldering with what looked suspiciously like anger, 'I think I'd better. Goodnight, Gay. And goodbye!'

Throughout the night, all Gay could think of, between restless spells of sleep, was the hardness in Luke's voice as he had left her. When he had said goodbye, he had sounded as if he really meant it this time.

The next day dragged. She was glad when the springlike weather brought increasing sales to the boutique, but that didn't seem to help the state of her heart. The dull, painful throb of it whenever she thought of Luke only confirmed her growing suspicions that she was falling in love with him. It was crazy, she kept telling herself, to imagine she was beginning to love a man she had known barely two weeks, yet something inside her wouldn't let her altogether deny it. Impatiently she tried to believe such feelings would soon die, especially as he wasn't going to see her again.

The next time he rang, three days later, she was so startled and agitated she found it difficult to find her breath. Why was he getting in touch with her, after making it clear he was never going to again? What sort of game was he playing? she asked herself fiercely.

'I wish you'd stop this!' she snapped. 'Anyway, who gave you my number?'

'I asked Mrs Douglas,' he rapped back. 'And I rang to make sure you hadn't been murdered. I'm presuming your brother is still away?'

'Yes, he is,' she answered coldly, 'and I'm still alive, as you can hear. What reason did you give for wanting my number?'

'I said my aunt might want to know more about the duck casserole.'

Gay didn't wonder he had got to the top! 'You think of everything, don't you?' she exclaimed, ringing off.

He came straight back, sounding furious. 'That's the second time you've hung up on me! I don't happen to like it.'

'I don't particularly like speaking to you, Mr Ashley,' she said tautly.

Ignoring this, he asked. 'Are you doing anything this evening?'

'If this is another invitation, you can stuff it!' she said insolently.

There was a moment's startled silence. No one's probably spoken to him like that in years, Gay thought, some of her impulsive anger fading.

'Forget it,' he replied stonily. This time it was he who hung up.

Well, she frowned unhappily, that's torn it! She looked in the directory, but he wasn't there, so she didn't have a hope of apologising. Yet why should she? Angry that such a thought had even crossed her mind, she tried to forget about it.

She had a shower and put on a light robe and wondered why her life should suddenly seem meaningless and empty. She had coffee made, in a desperate effort to cheer herself up, when the doorbell rang.

Lethargically she trailed to the door. It was a man her brother knew from down the street. 'What is it?' she smiled at him politely.

'I thought you might be lonely with Morris away,' he explained, with a leering grin.

Most of Morris's friends and acquaintances she liked, but this one she didn't. 'Sorry,' she said, lightly but firmly, 'I'm not lonely tonight.'

'You could be,' his breath smelled of drink as he came nearer, 'it's something that creeps up on you. You'd better invite me in.'

'No!' Feeling a warning twinge of apprehension, she tried to close the door, but his foot was in it.

'You look dressed for a visitor like me.'

'Please go away!' Suddenly she was really frightened. 'I'll tell Morris about this when he gets back, if you don't.'

'It might be worth a lecture at that,' he leered. 'I don't know what you have to be so hoity-toity about, anyway.'

'Is this man bothering you, Gay?' said a voice behind them.

Gay had never been so thankful to see anyone in her life. She even murmured a prayer of thanksgiving when she saw Luke. He must have come silently up the stairs while she'd been trying to defend herself. He wore no jacket, just a pullover and slacks, which did nothing to conceal the almost animal strength of his tall, lean body. After just one glance at him, her unwelcome visitor faded into the darkness with the startling suddenness of a spectre.

'Oh, Luke!' Gay almost fell against him with relief, but she was shaking and couldn't stop. With a grim curse he picked her up, carrying her inside and kicking the door shut behind him.

'You never learn, do you?' He seemed enraged beyond what was normal. 'Always in some kind of trouble over a man! If I hadn't arrived when I did, that character might have mauled you.'

'Put me down Luke, please!'

Ignoring the tears in her voice, he obliged. Almost throwing her into an armchair, he glanced around, trying to locate something to drink.

'However do you come to know anyone like that?' he demanded.

'Morris found him one evening in a bad way by the river,' Gay gasped, her words all seeming to be running together. 'Jim's all right when he's sober.'

'A fine way of showing his gratitude!'

'Yes, I know . . .' Luke was holding a glass of brandy against her lips and she grasped his hands anxiously as he seemed likely to pour it all down her throat at once. After a few sips the colour returned to her face and she pushed him away. 'Jim isn't so bad,' she insisted. 'He'll probably be around to apologise later.'

'You want to be here, later?'

Still trying to hide the effects of fright, she asked dazedly, 'Where else would I be?'

'You'll be at my place, with me.'

She almost jumped at his grim inflexibility. 'W-won't that be out of the frying pan and into the fire, Mr Ashley?'

'I'm not asking you to sleep with me,' he returned flatly, 'but you aren't staying here.' A muscle jerked in his cheek and his mouth tightened. 'When does your brother get back—if he is your brother?'

Gay straightened angrily, glaring up at him, her eyes blue flames. 'How dare you say things like that! You think Jim has a lousy mind, but yours is worse! You're . . .'

'All right,' he snapped, 'spare me, I've heard enough. It's your mind that needs washing out, not mine. I'm simply concerned for you and issuing a friendly invitation. And when your brother returns I want a word with him, to give him a piece of my mind!'

'He's due back tomorrow, but I'd rather you didn't.

He—he has a terrible temper,' Gay improvised wildly, for she didn't want them to meet. 'He'd think I'd been complaining, and it will be all right once he's here. No one would dare come near me then.'

'His reputation is such,' Luke drawled, 'that as soon as his back is turned, his so-called friends are ready to assault you?'

His open sarcasm made her flinch, while his concern for her—if that was what it was—made her wonder. His mouth had tightened and he was pale. It made her heartbeats quicken to think he might be even a little anxious.

'Come on,' he said brusquely, viewing the shabby flat with distaste. 'Whether you pack an overnight bag or not it's up to you, but I'll give you no more than five minutes.'

'You're forever rationing me with time!' she began heatedly.

'Gay!'

'Oh, all right!' she mumbled, fleeing to her bedroom, angry for giving in to him so easily yet unable to help herself.

His flat was everything a flat should be. The sheer elegance and comfort of it impressed Gay against her will.

'It makes Morris's look like a garbage bin!' she sighed.

Luke stared at her, his mouth compressed. 'You might pass for a lady, but your turn of speech often gives you away,' he commented.

'So all I need do is keep my mouth shut?'

Visibly he winced, his eyes cold with distaste. 'If you would,' he snapped, 'I'd be much obliged.'

'If I can't talk, what else is there to do?' she asked mildly, smiling at him maddeningly.

Suddenly his eyes weren't so cold any more and he was nearer, his hand on her arm, drawing her to him. 'I could think of something very enjoyable,' he teased, 'but you would have to release me from my foolish promise.'

His hands lightly touched her face and her traitorous heart began beating violently. Her eyes fell before the intentness of his gaze, but before she could escape he suddenly bent his head and took her mouth softly. The gentleness of it, the wave of sweetness it brought, caused her lips to move apart and respond blindly, while his hands sliding over her body made her head swim. Warmth seemed to touch every intimate, sentient part of her and she shuddered beneath an overwhelming rush of feeling. Soon, although the pressure of his mouth didn't deepen, she became breathless and he stopped kissing her reluctantly.

As they stared at each other in silence she became conscious of his iron control. His heart had thundered just as loudly as her own, his breath had come just as unevenly, but his greater experience enabled him to withdraw from such a situation with an ease which Gay envied. Because his feelings were not involved, his control of the merely physical was absolute and she felt like hitting him.

She had no intention of releasing him from any promise he had made not to molest her. It might be the only defence she had—from herself as much as him! Her cheeks were too hot, her pulses racing too crazily for her to pretend Luke didn't affect her.

She found the smouldering, waiting darkness in his eyes disturbing and pulled back. 'Aren't you going to show me around?' she asked.

For a moment he neither moved nor spoke, as if her deliberate flippancy jarred him. Then his hands fell to his sides, and he pushed one into his trouser pocket as he turned away.

'I'm not doing conducted tours,' he snapped, 'as well as being a good Samaritan. Would you like to go out?'

'Out?' she stammered, her eyes wide. 'At this time of night?'

'Don't be silly,' he said abruptly, 'it's barely ten

o'clock.' Then, glancing back at her uncertain face, he suggested with a little more patience, 'If you'd rather, I can make some coffee and you can look at the TV or read.'

'With you?' Gay tried to keep the eagerness from her voice.

'If you like,' he agreed grimly.

Gay nodded, feeling suddenly cheered. Strangely, at the moment, she couldn't think of anything she would like better. Despite the underlying tension which seemed always to be with them, she sensed also a certain sympathy, a tug of the senses which she had been aware of before. This, along with the nerves which prickled under her skin whenever he touched her, she found confusing yet enticing. It was like playing with fire and not expecting to get burnt. She had been out with other men, whom she had liked better, but had never felt this curious sense of attachment.

The feeling persisted as the evening wore on, as Luke's attitude perhaps puzzled her as much as her own. He was, she suspected, a sensuous man, who didn't always deny his sexual appetites. Yet he made no further attempt to make love to her. He played some Tchaikovsky, when she confessed to having seen *Swan Lake* several times. Then he played for himself a little Wagner, whom she had always found rather heavy.

'Perhaps it suits my present mood,' Luke replied with a sigh, making her endure it to the end.

They argued amiably, and when he laughed, which was surprisingly quite often, she felt it was something he hadn't done a lot of for some time. It was well after twelve when he suggested it was time she was in bed.

'I'll wake you early,' he promised, 'and have you home before your neighbours are up.'

Startled, that she hadn't thought of Morris or the flat or Jim for hours, Gay thanked Luke coolly. After he had shown her to her room, however, and said goodnight, she was conscious of her coolness dissolving into a sudden urgency of regret which she found almost frightening.

Luke woke her at six with a huge mug of tea. 'Come on, sleepyhead,' he said lightly, 'time you were out of there!'

He might have come deliberately early to see what she looked like when she first woke up, for he studied her closely, his silvery glance sliding over her tumbled hair, her uncertain eyes and flawless skin, then further down to where her nightdress clung briefly to the tender curves of her slim young body.

'You didn't get that for coppers,' he remarked dryly, expertly assessing.

It was a nightdress her mother had brought from Paris, for Gay's last birthday. 'It was a present,' she explained coldly, hoping this would suffice.

It didn't. His eyes glinting angrily, Luke came down on the bed. 'From whom?'

'S-someone I know . . .'

'So where is he now?' Luke asked roughly.

'Luke,' she protested, reaching blindly for her tea, which he had placed on the bedside cabinet, 'I refuse to spend time discussing a nightdress! I have to get home.'

Furiously he caught her hand before it could reach anything. Then, pulling it down to her side again, his hand slid up her arm to touch the narrow straps on her shoulders.

'How many men have seen you in this?' he asked tersely.

His question took her breath away. Her face burned as she retorted bitterly, 'How many do you think?'

'Suppose I find out?' he snapped, with a kind of understated fury.

All signs of humour had vanished from his hard face. He was dressed but without a jacket, his shirt open at the neck. The muscled strength of his broad chest, covered with dark hair, made Gay think of a ruthless pirate.

'Don't dare touch me!' she gasped, her heart beating heavily as, without compunction, he took her in his arms. His mouth was fierce on hers and she moaned weakly, clinging to him when she stopped fighting, while trying to hold on to her reeling senses. His touch inflamed her, destroying her will to resist. As his mouth brutally crushed hers with a kind of cruel hunger, everything else fled from her mind.

'Now are you going to tell me?' he whispered savagely, moments later, as he allowed her to draw a gasping breath.

His touch was torment, but she struggled to get away from him in vain. The roughness of his chest against the bareness of her own both hurt and excited her and she began to be aware of changes in him, of the suppressed desire in him, in the restless movements of his lean, powerful body and legs.

Tautly, as her limbs began melting against his, she cried, 'Who I've been with is my own business. Now will you please let me go!'

Ruthlessly, instead of doing so, Luke lowered his head, the anger in his eyes taking her apart as he silenced her inarticulate protests with his mouth. There was no tenderness in his kiss, only a determined insistence she was powerless to resist. Cruelly he tore her nightdress until the fragile silk ripped in his hands—hands which grasped at the soft skin underneath until she moaned with pain. Her frantic struggles ceased as terror swept through her. She felt herself swept by flames as her body caught fire and went limp under his.

When he pushed her contemptuously away, she was so dizzy she couldn't move, although she seemed to be shaking all over. With fumbling hands she gripped the sheets tightly, trying not to shame herself by fainting. Luke's features blurred in front of her, the room swung slightly. Then slowly her vision cleared so she could more easily discern the hardness of his eyes, the rigid firmness of his mouth.

'I'm sorry if you got more than you bargained for,' he said indifferently, 'but it was nothing more than a kiss.'

'It was hateful!' Her voice caught on a sob as she glared at him.

'You're sure?'

'Stop taunting me!' She brushed a tear from her eye, desperately trying to hide it.

'Wasn't it as much your fault?' he asked derisively, his glance going from her damp cheeks to her torn nightdress. 'You taunted me with that. I'll replace it, of course, but the next time come decently attired.'

'There won't be a next time!' she whispered, knowing she would never trust herself within miles of him again.

CHAPTER FIVE

THEY ate bacon and eggs together in Luke's streamlined kitchen while the sky lightened in the east to let fingers of dawn push through. Gay made a pretence of eating, but in the end her jumping nerves defeated her and she pushed her plate away.

The silence between them, not surprisingly, was taut after the emotion and anger they had shared upstairs. Gay was aware of Luke staring at her from time to time, but kept her own eyes fixed stubbornly on the table.

After they had finished, he carried the dishes to the sink but refused to let Gay touch them. He would do them later, he said. He had already told her how he had loaned the couple he employed to his aunt, until she was able to make her own domestic arrangements.

'Come on, Gay, I'll get you home,' he said.

Gay became aware of him glancing at the clock. Rising stiffly to her feet, she followed him obediently.

The street was quiet and she suddenly realised it was Saturday. 'Will you go to your office this morning?' she asked suddenly.

'No,' he replied coldly.

'What will you do?' she persisted, a wistfulness she wasn't conscious of in her voice.

He glanced at her impatiently, as they drove from the garage, as if he wished she hadn't asked. 'I'm going away for the weekend.'

With—Lily?'

'Yes,' he frowned. 'Her people are entertaining—a house party.'

'How nice,' Gay sighed enviously, thinking, despite their differences, how nice it would have been to have been able to spend a whole weekend with him.

'I don't think you would care for that sort of thing,' he observed, obviously thinking she was referring to the house party.

Gay stared at her hands, which were clenched tight. 'Are you going to propose to Miss Dalmonte this weekend?'

'It's none of your damned business, but I may do,' he replied harshly.

Gay went pale. 'I—understand.'

'Stop saying that!' he exploded softly, his knuckles white on the steering wheel. 'You don't understand one damned thing but your own point of view.'

'So I'm selfish . . .?'

'I suppose it isn't your fault,' he said grimly. 'I expect you've been brought up to grab, without a thought for anyone else. It breeds a typical kind of self-centredness.'

The force of his tirade bent her head dejectedly, but it wasn't his wrath so much as the weekend stretching emptily ahead that made her unhappy. Brushing back a gleaming swathe of thick hair from off her forehead, she tried to move her shoulders in a careless shrug, as she straightened. What did she care how many women Luke Ashley chose to propose to? Or what he did? She had plenty of friends, hadn't she, whom she could ring up.

She said nothing more until they reached the flat. Luke grunted something, but she looked straight ahead, unaware of his glance lingering on the pure and lovely lines of her averted profile.

Every day of the following week Gay brought a copy of *The Times*, but there was no announcement of any engagement. Eventually, unable to restrain herself a moment longer, she rang the offices of Ashley Industries, but was repulsed firmly at every attempt she made to contact Luke.

'I'm sorry,' she was told, 'Mr Ashley never sees anyone without an appointment.'

An appointment? Gay thought rapidly, sweat beading

her brow, making her hands clammy. If she gave her own name he would never consent to seeing her.

'Would you please tell him that Mrs Douglas—Mrs David Douglas—is in trouble,' she improvised wildly. 'It's extremely important that I speak to him personally.'

The voice hesitated, then asked her doubtfully to wait. 'Mr Ashley will see you at three this afternoon,' the voice returned a few minutes later. 'I'll inform the commissionaire. I hope you can provide some proper means of identification?'

Katrina might be on the high seas. Heaven help me, Gay thought, if Luke should try to get in touch with her or David! The commissionare appeared to know about her appointment. After frisking her lightly he let her through and with fast beating heart she was borne to the top floor in the lift.

She only began trembling in earnest when she was actually waiting to see Luke. It was just after three when his secretary said he would see her now.

Unsteadily Gay rose to her feet trying not to notice the woman's interested stare. Gay, in turn, stared at the door of Luke's office as though it were Mount Everest and she had never climbed before. Whatever would she say to him? She had been so agitated and in such a hurry, she hadn't rehearsed anything. How on earth was she to explain to a man she'd only known a few weeks that she had gone to such ridiculous lengths simply to find out about his probable engagement? He would never understand. Dear heavens, she didn't understand herself, so how could she expect Luke to?

Aware of his secretary's enquiring eyebrows rising higher, Gay decided there was nothing for it but to brazen it out.

Forcing strength into weak legs, she took a step forward, but before she could make any real progress Luke appeared himself.

'Mrs Douglas?' he began, and stopped, a slightly

stunned expression on his face. 'Gay!' He stared at her abruptly. 'What on earth's going on? I expected Mrs Douglas. What are you doing here?'

'I know you expected Mrs Douglas.' Gay swallowed and cast an agonised glance at his secretary. 'I—I knew you wouldn't see me, so I pretended to be her. Could I please speak to you in private?'

Her hands were shaking, she was pale, but if Luke noticed her distress he ignored it. He frowned, his eyes hard, and made no attempt to invite her into his office.

Apparently impervious, in this instance, to his secretary's curiosity, he rapped out, 'You had no business tricking your way in here, Gay. What the devil do you want?'

Gay's breath seemed to be trapped painfully in her breast. When she found it again she uttered the first thing to enter her head, for of course she couldn't ask him about Lily in front of an audience. 'You promised me a job,' she whispered.

'You must be mad!' he exclaimed, his his eyes slating her. 'Do you mean to tell me you've come here, wasting both my time and Miss Carson's, because of something you must have imagined in the first place? I have no intention of employing you.'

'Oh, but——' Gay began.

Miss Carson intervened, with a purr of satisfaction. 'Shall I get someone to remove her, Mr Ashley?'

'Mind your own bloody business!' he replied.

'It wasn't just that, Luke,' Gay gabbled, as Miss Carson fell back, looking mortally offended. 'I wondered if you and—and Miss Dal . . .'

'Will you shut up!' Luke's teeth snapped, fury making his silvery eyes glitter like icicles.

Feeling physically sick, Gay knew he would never forgive her. He would believe she had deliberately created this undignified scene. Suddenly her eyes filled with tears. 'I'm sorry, Luke,' she gasped, as the tears overflowed, 'I'll go.'

'No, Gay,' he snapped, 'you'll do nothing of the sort!'

Unheeding, and terrified of the harshness of his voice, she turned and fled. Panic lent wings to her stumbling feet as a crash behind her seemed to indicate violence barely held in check.

'Gay!' Luke called. 'Wait a minute! Come back!'

She didn't listen. Blood was pounding in her ears so heavily she scarcely heard. Only vaguely was she conscious of his voice begging her to stop, of people raising curious faces. Somehow she found the lift and the right button and raced from the building as if the devil himself was after her.

She didn't return to the flat straight away. Morris wasn't there, he was doing another job abroad, but in the unlikely event of Luke following her to exact vengeance, that might be the first place he would look.

Gay felt she was going mad and she must have walked miles trying to get rid of the sensation. There must be something wrong with her, otherwise how could she have acted as she had done? It was dark when she found herself near the river and she cried until her eyes were red and swollen. She had discovered what was wrong with her, but she only felt worse. What a stupid little fool she was to have fallen in love with a man who refused to even acknowledge such an emotion. A man who had frankly revealed that if he married, he would only marry a wife who could help him socially.

A smothered moan escaped Gay's dry lips as she stared at the dark, forbidding water. Luke had some feeling for her. No man bothered taking a girl out, whatever his excuse, if he wasn't in some measure attracted. But Luke's feelings were only skin deep. He had no love to offer. If she hadn't made such a fool of herself today, she suspected he might have asked her to consider having an affair with him. If he wasn't already engaged to Lily Dalmonte.

Thankful, at least, for being spared the humiliation of such an offer, Gay trailed bitterly back to the flat. It would be empty and lonely, but there was nowhere else to go.

Her head was down, her feet dragging wearily, when Luke's car swept round the corner, narrowly missing her as she began blindly to cross the road.

'Gay!' he flung open the door, leaning over to almost drag her inside. 'What in heaven's name do you think you're doing now? I could have killed you!'

'I——' she was aware of the intentness of his gaze but couldn't look at him, 'I didn't expect to see you.'

'If it hadn't been me it might have been some other motorist,' he snapped, obviously modifying his language with difficulty. 'Where have you been? I've been looking for you everywhere.'

Still she refused to look at him. Her heart was racing crazily, it took her all her time to speak. 'Why should you have been looking for me? I thought you wouldn't want to see me again, not after this afternoon.'

Luke sighed, moving restlessly, then put a hand on her cheek, turning her face towards him. As she sucked in a tortured breath he moved a finger over the taut line of her chin to softly caress the trembling shape of her lips. The feeling it triggered off was unbearable, and with a mute little cry of protest she jerked her head away.

It was Luke's turn to draw breath, but his was harsher, a curious rasping sound, as though her sudden withdrawal didn't please him. 'We'd better talk, you and I. Is your brother in?'

'No,' she replied without thinking, 'he's in France.'

'Long may he stay there,' Luke rejoined curtly, 'for the next hour at least.'

Inside the flat he secured the door. 'We'd better take precautions. Your drunken friend whom your brother mistakenly saved from the river might feel like calling, and I'm not feeling particularly sociable.'

Gay scarcely heard him. She was intent on getting to her bedroom, hoping to repair the ravages of copious tears before Luke noticed.

She might have known he was naturally geared for such moves and too quick for her. Before she could escape he had grasped her arm, jerking her round to face him. At the sight of her face in a good light, his own darkened.

'Gay,' he rasped, his eyes suddenly blazing, 'why do you do such things? You're so impulsive and you only hurt yourself.'

'To act without thinking is something you wouldn't understand,' she flung at him incoherently, ready to faint from the pressure of his detaining hands.

'That's where you could easily be mistaken,' he snapped tersely, his long lean fingers impatiently brushing the thick strands of silken hair from off her forehead and hot cheeks. 'Don't think you're the only one occasionally at the mercy of their emotions, but don't misunderstand me, Gay. I don't want you hurt like this again.'

Her skin, which was hot because of tears, seemed scorched where he touched it. It was impossible to read entirely what he was thinking. He looked grim and she wondered why he continued to hold her. She moved restlessly, biting her lip as he examined her face thoroughly. 'You mean you don't want me visiting your office again?'

For an instant he frowned, but merely said, 'Not if it means such an upset. What my staff are saying and thinking, I can't imagine. Nor do I particularly want to.'

'Is that all that bothers you?' she asked wildly.

'No,' he returned steadily, but added nothing more.

Some of the shock Gay had sustained that afternoon was still with her. She was trembling right through, not all the tears she had wept had got rid of it. Vaguely she realised this and knew she must make an effort to pull herself together. No good would come of sniping at Luke—he was always too much for her.

'I'm sorry,' she gulped, aware he deserved an apology. She had invaded his office without a thought for anyone but herself. If she had been cool and sensible he might have forgiven her, but in making such a scene she had clearly transgressed beyond all hope of forgiveness. 'I'm sorry, Luke,' she repeated, this time hopelessly.

Suddenly, surprisingly, he exclaimed, 'I don't really care what my staff are thinking, Gay. It's you——' He hesitated, glancing away from her hurt face as if he didn't care for the sight of it. 'I don't like you tearing yourself to pieces like this. It makes me feel responsible.'

'You don't have to.' Her voice came cooler with a little dredged-up pride, then cracked humiliatingly. 'After all, you made it clear from the beginning how you felt about me.'

Abruptly he turned away, as though for some reason he didn't trust himself near her any longer. 'It's as well you remember,' he rejoined grimly. 'We can't take each other seriously, Gay.'

She sighed unhappily, letting her eyes follow him wistfully. He sounded so reasonable she tried not to resent that he was so immune from the turbulent emotions which continually plagued her. As he turned back to her, she tried to take comfort from the fact that he didn't seem so angry any more. His eyes were silvery dark as they rested on her. If she hadn't known better she might even have believed they held concern.

A curious shiver went through her as he took hold of her jacket, slipping it from her shoulders with gentle hands. 'You'd better go and have a shower, Gay. You look all in. While you're busy, I'll make some coffee. I could do with some myself.'

In the bathroom which, like Morris's kitchen, was surprisingly well equipped, she stripped and showered, letting the water soothe her aching limbs. Then, after dressing again in a silky blouse and skirt, she ran a quick comb through her hair and went back to Luke.

'That didn't take long.' His dark brows rose as he poured her a mug of steaming coffee.

'I didn't bother much or it might have done.' She drank the coffee gratefully, without confessing that she had hurried deliberately so as to leave herself no time to think. Wiping the back of a hand over her bare mouth, she put the mug back but on the table.

'Feeling better?' Luke enquired.

'Yes, thank you.' She spoke like a child, keeping her eyes lowered, for fear he might see the misery which still lingered.

'We have to talk, I think.' Taking her arm, he drew her firmly back to the living-room. Guiding her to the settee, he sat down beside her. 'I believe you owe me some kind of explanation about today—why you came to my office in the first place.'

'I told you,' she whispered painfully, her young face strained, 'I wanted to find out if you were engaged. There was nothing in the newspapers and I couldn't remember where you lived. You aren't in the directory, either.'

'Engaged?' he frowned, his eyes narrowed.

'You said last weekend you might be,' she cried, with sharp impatience.

'Oh, that? Well, I'm not,' he assured her curtly.

He sounded suddenly like a man with limits, and Gay thought she knew why. 'Did she turn you down?'

'I didn't ask her.'

'You didn't ask her?' A raging fury almost swamped Gay at his indifference. He had left her to guess, to suffer, unheedingly! 'You could have given me a ring,' she accused him frantically.

'There was no reason why I should,' he exclaimed, dousing the flames of her anger coldly. 'For God's sake stop being so childish!'

'I'm not a child!' she flashed back, indignation overwhelming her.

'You are in lots of ways, and I'm a good deal older. When you came to my office I ought to have shaken you until you came to your senses. We can't all indulge in foolish infatuations.'

Her anger evaporating as quickly as it had risen, Gay stared at him dully. So that was what he thought of the feelings she had for him! He considered it a foolish infatuation. She felt terribly hurt. She was almost twenty—surely no child, and all she wanted was to be able to love him, freely and for ever. But, because of rules, the life he had mapped out for himself, nothing could ever come of it.

'I'm sorry, Luke,' she muttered. 'You must be right.' Ready to sink through the floor that he had guessed her feelings so easily, she sought to deny them convincingly. 'Do you know, I really did think I fancied you, but if I did, this afternoon has certainly cured me.'

'Really?' He was masculine enough to take up the challenge she had unwittingly thrown down. When he moved closer, she was vaguely aware of having made a mistake. His silvery eyes were trained on her, nearly taking her breath away, while all she wanted to do was coolly ignore him. As he took hold of her bright coloured spots appeared on her cheeks and she felt like bursting into tears again. How could she allow any man to throw her into such absolute chaos?

Before she could guess his intention, he had drawn her roughly into his arms. 'How—cured?' he murmured lazily, his mouth only a breath away.

For a man who didn't want her he was acting oddly—unless it was another kind of punishment? 'Oh, no!' she cried, conscious of a sudden burning desire beginning to pound along her veins. Her heart thudded, but he took no notice of her anguished little plea. His arms tightened and his mouth came down on hers, crushing all resistance, making her respond until she was returning his kisses with increasing urgency. She was lost in a tide of relentless desire which threatened to sweep away any barrier she might raise against it. This was Luke and she loved him, the man who wanted and then rejected her in turn.

As this reminded her harshly of the pain she had suffered, and still would, when he remembered she wasn't for him, she tried to push him away.

Wrenching her mouth from his, she gasped, 'Let go of me, Luke, please!'

For an answer, he thrust a hand inside the loosened front of her blouse, lightly brushing her warm skin. The sensation was devastating. It was breathtaking, such a deep surge of passion from the mere touch of his fingers. Again her resistance crumbled as he continued making love to her and her arms went helplessly around his neck.

Yearning drove her to get closer and closer, yet, as he pressed her savagely against the muscular hardness of his body, alarm bells began ringing in Gay's mind. 'Please,' she murmured distractedly, as he lowered his mouth to her breasts, 'Luke, you'd better stop.'

He raised his head, shaking it absently. 'Why?' he demanded huskily.

On a half sob, she whispered, 'You know why . . . I mean nothing to you.'

'You drive me mad, while other women leave me cold,' he muttered thickly, his eyes glittering down on her, obviously hating her because of this. 'You only have to look at me,' he groaned, 'and I'm on fire. You make me burn—don't you understand?'

She wasn't sure that she did, but then she didn't seem sure of anything any more. If she was tense, so was he, his features tightly controlled but full of a desire he made no attempt to hide. His mouth returned to hers and, as his kisses deepened, Gay felt herself growing dizzy. Her pulses ran riot, merging with the throbbing thunder of Luke's heart as her body melted helplessly against his.

'Love me,' she breathed against his hot, demanding

mouth, begging now for what she had just rejected. 'Please, Luke, love me!'

His hands, around her narrow waist and in her hair, tightened convulsively, then she felt him stiffen—and suddenly she was alone on the settee.

'I'm sorry,' he muttered huskily, thrusting her away from him as he got to his feet, 'I can't.'

For a moment Gay was too bewildered to feel anything else but cheated. She was young and this was the first time she had known real passion. 'Luke?' she whispered, uncertainly, her voice full of unconscious longing.

'Stop it, Gay,' he snapped grimly. 'I'm going now. You'd better lock the door behind me—and be thankful I came to my senses in time.'

Gay stared at him, the hectic colour in her cheeks fading, to leave her as pale as he was. She had wanted to surrender in his arms, regardless of the consequences, but he hadn't wanted her. Wasn't it written on every hard line of his face? He had merely been amusing himself, curious as to how far she would let him go. Now that he had found out, he had lost interest.

Until today she hadn't even guessed how ruthless Luke could be. She had thought he had a softer side to his nature, but she realised now she was mistaken. He might be sensual and passionate, but never to such an overwhelming degree that he lost control. Tonight, she felt instinctively, with an inward shrinking, he had been carrying out some kind of experiment.

Feeling deathly cold, she forced herself to ask casually, 'Will I be seeing you again?'

'No!' he replied, almost violently. 'I went through enough this afternoon looking for you to recognise that you aren't good for me. We aren't good for each other, Gay, and we both know it. I shan't be coming back. This time I mean it . . .'

During the following weeks Gay realised she had never

known what true unhappiness was. She was consumed by misery and despair, until she wasn't sure that she could go on living. Always, before, Luke had said goodbye as though he meant it, then got in touch again. It took her some time, many agonising hours, to realise that this time he didn't mean to. The telephone didn't ring—there were no messages, just a bleak, frightening silence, which seemed to grow worse by the hour. Sometimes she felt so numb she was sure she would never feel anything again, yet when indirectly she heard or saw something of Luke she was conscious of searing pain. Yet none of this was quite as bad as the sheer apprehension that attacked her on the day he came with Lily Dalmonte to the boutique in Chelsea, in the King's Road.

'Money, darling!' Alice burst into the back premises where Gay was trying to grab a cup of tea. They had been extra busy all day and she was tired. It was almost time to go home and she didn't feel curious. Julie referred to all her best customers as 'money', so her assistants would know they were important and act with extra tolerance. Usually in a crowded shop, this one brief word was enough. Alice believed in flattering all her clients, but especially the rich ones, and they always came back.

'Do you want me to see to her?' Gay asked.

'No, I'll go, darling, don't worry,' Alice smiled. 'It's just little Miss Masham from Kent. She's upstairs in Accessories, but finish your tipple, love. You know how she likes having a poke around and hates being harried.'

Alice slipped out again and a few minutes later Gay dutifully followed. She was just about to go to the top floor, where the accessories were kept, when, on passing the salon door, she saw Luke. He was lounging on one of the Regency sofas beside the window. At that exact moment he turned his head and their eyes met.

'Luke!' She wasn't sure if she spoke his name or if

it froze on the end of her tongue. She went cold all over, and Luke looked frozen too. The effort she made to pull herself together seemed to hurt terribly, but she was just about to try and speak again when Miss Dalmonte swept into the salon wearing one of Alice's latest, most exquisite creations.

'Just the thing for a honeymoon, don't you think, Luke darling?' Lily gushed, not noticing Gay, transfixed in the doorway.

Gay swayed. She knew she must have turned white, she felt so shocked. Luke stared at Gay while Alice enthusiastically agreed with Lily and suggested a minor alteration.

Suddenly Gay could bear it no longer. She felt so awful she thought she might faint. Wrenching her eyes away from Luke's narrowed yet piercing gaze, she stumbled back the way she had come. Miss Masham would have to wait.

Unsteadily she retreated to the workroom, relieved to find no one there. So Luke had settled his future at last. He had talked long enough of marrying Lily, and now Lily was talking of honeymoons and had him following her around like a pet lamb. She must be buying her trousseau. Luke wouldn't have to pay for it, of course, as Lily's father was wealthy—he must have millions! He would probably be willing to pay anything to get his daughter off his hands after all this time, with the added bonus of a brilliant son-in-law. Luke certainly had his head screwed on the right way—there was no denying that!

Bitterly Gay scribbled a note for Alice and hastily left the boutique. Luke had stared at her as though she were a stranger. He had recognised her, all right, but he hadn't even said hello. He had gone pale but, Gay was sure, with anger. Considering the opinion he had of her character, he had probably feared she had some intention of embarrassing him. Well, good luck to him, she thought bitterly, collapsing on her bed when she reached the flat, in a painful flood of tears.

After a restless, unhappy night, Gay was glad to rise early. Unable to sit still, she began a positive storm of cleaning. This morning she felt years older and disillusioned. She ached with misery whenever she thought of Luke, but refused to lie in bed brooding about him. She must be sensible and try and forget him. Perhaps, she decided bleakly, she should find another man to help her do this.

Morris, as usual, objected to such a flurry of early morning activity. As she vacuumed the living-room he appeared, half asleep, in his dressing-gown. 'For the love of Mike, Gay,' he groaned, 'will you shut that damned thing off! If you must do something, why not make a cup of tea? I'm bushed!'

Gay obeyed, but reluctantly. 'You shouldn't stay out all night, then you might feel more civilised,' she said tartly.

'When I want your advice I'll ask for it!' he snapped.

In the kitchen, Gay raised feathery brows as she filled mugs of tea. 'What's wrong? Julie?'

'Not really.' He stared into his cup, as if trying to read his future. 'No problem there.'

'Because she'd fall in your lap at one beckon of your little finger!'

Morris glanced at Gay in astonishment, running a rueful hand over a rasping chin, 'You're very sharp this morning, infant. I'm actually considering asking her to marry me.'

Gay gasped incredulously at his patronising tone. Did all men imagine they were lords of creation, able to treat women as they liked? 'You go on considering much longer, brother,' she snapped, 'and she'll be off with somebody else.'

'Why should she,' Morris frowned, 'when she loves me?'

'Oh, forget I said that,' Gay sighed shortly. 'You go ahead. Perhaps she might be able to reform you.'

'Do you wonder why I hesitate?' Morris muttered moodily. 'You women are all the same. If I married Julie—and I haven't actually decided to, mind you—she'd be like you in no time. Trying to tidy me up, domesticate me, make me do things her way.'

'So—no way had you better marry her,' Gay said angrily. 'I shouldn't think of marrying anyone if I were you, not until you meet a girl you consider special. If you think Julie's the same as everyone else I'd say you didn't love her. If you loved her . . .' she trailed off, startled to hear a sob in her voice, 'you wouldn't care who she was, and you'd be willing to do anything to please her.'

Morris stared at his sister in astonishment for a long moment, then, his eyes suddenly narrowing, he abruptly changed the subject. 'Jim's been telling me about a man who's been coming around while I've been away. Is he right, have you got a—er—new friend, or is he just imagining things?'

He must mean Luke. Gay coloured faintly, then went pale. 'If Jim didn't drink, he wouldn't imagine so much! This time, though, he's right. I have been out with someone, but it's all over . . .'

'Really?' Morris studied her with the thoughtfulness he was capable of when he wasn't immersed in his work, then again he changed the subject abruptly. 'You've got beautiful lines to your face, girl. What wouldn't I give if only the parents . . . Oh, lord!' he broke off with an impatient flick of his wrist, 'that reminds me. I had Patricia on the blower yesterday, before I went out—before you were in. She's sprained her ankle or something and wants you over there.'

'Oh, no!' Gay gazed at him in consternation. Morris always called her mother Patricia—a kind of mutual arrangement. 'How bad is she? Why didn't you tell me sooner?'

'Apart from the ankle, she's fine, I believe, so don't panic,' he grunted. 'I'm sorry, love,' he added viewing

Gay's stricken face more remorsefully, 'I meant to leave a message, but I'd so much on I forgot. Anyway, she said today would do, if you can manage it. I said there was nothing to stop you, so it's all arranged. Nigel will meet you.'

It was all arranged, conveniently, Gay suspected, from Morris's point of view. He was off that very morning on yet another overseas assignment, so the flat was locked up and they left together, just over an hour later. Morris, always more efficient than he appeared to be, had booked her flight and insisted on seeing her off. Gay appreciated this, but not the quick glances of concern he was suddenly casting in her direction. Because of this—and Luke—she was glad to leave London behind and welcomed the sunshine of Paris.

Nigel Trent, her father's aide, met her at the airport. He was in love with her, which was one of the reasons she didn't come to Paris very often. Yet he was a nice young man and very personable, and she had often thought he would make a good husband. If it hadn't been for Luke she might have eventually accepted him. Nigel had been proposing regularly since she was eighteen and sometimes she felt terribly guilty that she couldn't bring herself to say yes. Glancing at him sideways, as they drove into the city, she realised she could never love him, now she had met Luke. Comparing him with Luke was like comparing strong drink with water. Nigel didn't even make her pulse beat a fraction faster, while Luke, without effort, could make it go completely wild.

She remained in Paris three weeks before returning with her family to London. Her mother's ankle recovered, but until it did Gay stood in for her at various functions. Though she was far from completely confident, her youth and beauty made up for a certain lack of experience. Her father was delighted with her, having previously despaired of her reluctance to have anything much to do with the social commitments which were all part of his job. Gay let him think she had changed, for how could she tell him she was so miserable over Luke that she didn't really care what she did? Besides, wasn't being anywhere, doing anything, better than being in London, where his presence was a constant reminder of everything she couldn't have?

CHAPTER SIX

NIGEL returned to London with them. Gay had dined and been out with him several times and their friendship must appear to be growing, for she knew her parents were secretly hoping something more permanent might come of it. Gay was aware that her paleness and lack of vitality puzzled her mother, but by the time they left Paris she was convinced she was looking better.

In London she lived with her parents, but only, she insisted, until she found a place of her own. Alice had been forced to find another assistant and Gay decided not to approach her again but to look for something else. A living-in job in the country appealed to her, but she wasn't sure exactly what, and was in no hurry to make up her mind. A curious apathy seemed to hold her in its grip and somehow she couldn't manage to fight her way out of it.

Her mother was anxious, then cross. They were on their way to an important reception. Gay had done her best to get out of it, but in the end, because her father had been bitterly disappointed, she had given in.

'I can't understand you, darling,' her mother said impatiently. 'Any other girl . . .'

'I know,' Gay interrupted tensely, 'any other girl would lap it up, and I'm a continual source of disappointment. That's why I have to find somewhere else to live. Then Daddy wouldn't be able to insist I was one of the family and must come along. I don't mind sometimes,' she added hastily, 'but not every evening. I must have a life of my own.'

'But you're one of the family!' her mother protested. 'And I refuse to believe you are wholly cut out to live on your own. Why don't you marry Nigel?' she suggested brightly. 'Your father would like that.'

'Don't my wishes count?' Gay smiled rather wryly.

'Yes, of course they do,' Patricia assured her. 'I was only trying to be helpful. I certainly wouldn't dream of trying to persuade you to marry any man unless you loved him, but Nigel is nice and I think you could be happy.'

Her mother was sweet. Gay sighed ruefully as they left the taxi and went to join her father. It was because her mother was so nice that she made no real effort to wriggle out of functions like this. As she stood dutifully behind her parents as they received their guests, her eyes swept the glittering company dully. It had been a week of important trade delegations, culminating in a sort of grand finale. There were many women, all beautifully dressed, with attentive escorts. People who were obviously enjoying themselves, finding plenty to talk about.

Gay, watching them absently, was conscious of a fleeting envy. Why couldn't she be enjoying herself too, instead of failing miserably? If only she hadn't fallen in love with Luke, how easy it might have been. It was then that she saw him. He was alone, having just arrived, and was walking steadily towards the reception area.

Horrified, Gay stepped back. She hadn't even glanced at the guest list. Now she wished she had. Apart from that, if she'd only stopped to think she might have guessed Luke would be here. Swallowing hard, she looked again. He was approaching with his usual catlike tread, a big man and, in full evening dress, devastatingly handsome.

Gay's heart leapt. He hadn't seen her and she had an urgent desire to disappear before he did. Out of the corner of her eye she spotted Nigel and tried to signal hurriedly, but it was too late. Her mother, as if guessing her intention, caught her arm, drawing her forward even as Luke was speaking to Gay's father before turning to his wife.

'Lady Fenton!' he smiled charmingly.

When Patricia introduced them, Gay saw Luke visibly start. His face went pale and tightened, so much so that the bones seemed to harden and stand out.

'Don't you think I've got a beautiful daughter, Luke?' she heard her father saying proudly as Luke held out his hand and she was forced to put her own in it. 'Would you care for a drink?' he asked, keeping hold of her hand as more people came up behind them.

'Oh—no. I'm sorry,' she stammered, her hand trembling within the cruel grasp he kept on it.

'Go with Mr Ashley, darling,' her mother murmured in her ear, 'I don't think there's much more you can do here.'

Reluctantly Gay allowed herself to be drawn along. She was aware of Luke's glittering eyes and of her own refusal to meet them. His silent disapproval and anger was filling her with fear and she tried to control a hysterical inclination to tear herself away from him and run. Why should she feel so frightened? She had done nothing to be ashamed of. She hadn't left Luke, it had been the other way round. If he was about to give her a lecture on deceit, then couldn't she accuse him of being a despicable snob?

'I don't want a drink!' she protested, as he half dragged her towards the bar. There were waiters with trays of drinks, but these he ignored, obviously seeking more privacy than was afforded here.

'Perhaps you'd rather dance?' his voice grated.

'No,' she whispered hoarsely, 'not that either.'

'Good,' he rejoined silkily, 'then you won't mind if we go elsewhere?'

'Elsewhere?' she croaked helplessly.

'We have to talk.'

'Do we?' She glanced away from him, trying to find Nigel again, feeling like a ship in a storm searching desperately for an anchor. 'I—I can't go anywhere with you,' she stammered desperately, 'I'm here with someone else.'

Luke grunted. 'I noticed Nigel Trent hovering. How well do you know him?' he asked savagely, her faint flush appearing to goad him.

Incredulously, Gay stared at him. 'You have a nerve, haven't you! Weeks ago you walked out of my life, you didn't want to see me again. Now you think you can come back as if nothing had happened and begin dictating about my friends!'

'I tried to walk out!' he muttered.

Nothing he said was making sense, and she didn't try to understand that, either. Clenching her hands in tight balls to stop them trembling, she cried unsteadily, 'Well, I can't walk out tonight. I promised my parents I'd stay and stay I must. You'll just have to find some other means of amusing yourself.'

For a moment his dark features were contorted with grim anger. 'All right,' he agreed tersely, 'I'll give you an hour, then we'll leave. You can make what excuses you like, so long as you come with me.'

'And if I don't?' she asked defiantly, for he seemed to be giving her an ultimatum.

Luke's eyes glinted coldly. 'Perhaps your father wouldn't be so proud of you if he were to learn of your weakness for married men. Does he know about Douglas?'

Completely stunned, Gay went pale, then coloured wildly. Horrified, she stared at the hard face of her tormentor. It hadn't occurred to her, but where David was concerned her hands might still be tied. If Luke were merely to mention his suspicions to her parents they would think it a huge joke and naturally tell him the truth. And if, after all that had gone before, Luke was to learn that David was her cousin, and she had never worked for Katrina, he might, with some justification, conclude that he had been made a fool of and sack David. Gay felt caught in a trap of her own making and the knowledge shook her. Where, today, would David find another such job? At all costs, she mustn't be the cause of him losing this one.

She met Luke's cruel stare and looked away quickly. 'You're very shrewd!' she exclaimed bitterly.

'So?' he snapped.

Suddenly her defences collapsed. 'You win,' she said tonelessly. 'I'll do anything if you promise to keep quiet about the Douglases?'

'I will,' he added scornfully, his eyes full of contempt, 'If you come to my flat we can forget about the Douglases.'

'All right,' she agreed unhappily, thrusting back her hair with unsteady fingers.

Nigel came up to them. 'My dance, Gay, I believe?' He glanced at Luke curiously.

Luke warned curtly, 'The next one is mine, Gay.'

'I had no idea you knew Luke Ashley.' Nigel frowned suspiciously as he took her in his arms. 'How did you meet him?'

'Daddy knows him,' she hedged, shrinking from a longer explanation.

Nigel, fortunately, accepted this, appearing quite willing to forget Luke. Drawing Gay closer, he said eagerly, 'You're looking lovely, this evening, darling. I wish you'd marry me. We like each other and get on well enough.'

'Oh, Nigel!' she shook her head at him wryly. A few weeks ago that might have satisfied her, but since then she had learnt a lot. A few weeks ago she might have considered the warm affection she shared with Nigel quite sufficient for a successful marriage. Now she knew better. 'I'm sorry,' she faltered, despondently, 'I'm afraid I can't marry you.'

'Why not?' he asked bleakly.

'Because I don't love you,' Gay replied reluctantly, hating to hurt him. Nigel was nice, he didn't deserve to be hurt.

'You could learn to love me.'

'No . . .'

'You sound very sure,' he retorted darkly, adding, astutely for Nigel, 'No one could be so sure. Not unless they were in love with someone else?' When Gay flushed, he exclaimed angrily, 'I see!'

Rather than argue about it, Gay merely shook her head, trying to convey that he didn't understand at all. 'I'm sorry,' she whispered.

'Forget it,' he replied wryly, 'It's my own fault if I feel hurt. You don't have to spell it out. I've known for a long time that you didn't love me, but because I thought there was no one else, I suppose I kept on hoping.'

That Nigel was being so reasonable only made her feel worse, and she was strangely relieved when their dance ended and Luke was there.

Luke steered her away, with only a brief nod for her previous partner. 'Are you having an affair with him?' he demanded.

The anger in his voice hurt, but she tried to ignore it. 'I don't have to answer that,' she snapped, feeling mortally wounded, 'nor will I go anywhere with you if you can only insult me!'

'Perhaps insults are all you deserve,' he jeered harshly.

She glanced up at his dark, angry face dispiritedly. 'You always did have a poor opinion of me, Luke, and it hasn't changed. All things considered, I can't think what we can have to talk about.'

'We needn't do a lot of talking,' he muttered ambiguously, 'not now that I've discovered everything about you, but there are things, important things, we have to discuss.'

He pulled her closer on the dance floor, regardless of any attention they might be attracting. They moved together, their thighs touching, his cheek surprisingly against her hair. It seemed mockery, yet she was conscious of pleasure. She was also conscious of the hardness of his lean body all the way down. His hands were moulding her to him, crushing her against the hard muscles of his chest, making her aware of herself in a way that made her catch her breath. He was arousing her deliberately, she suspected, his movements controlled but very sensuous. She would do well to remember his experience was far beyond her own, yet all she seemed able to think of was how much she had missed him.

The shiver of delight which ran down her spine as his lips lightly touched the softness of her cheek was so fierce it almost frightened her.

Feeling her tremble, Luke said mockingly. 'Are you going to deny that you like me?'

'I don't intend having an affair with you, if that's what you mean,' she exclaimed.

'It's not,' he replied grimly, his voice much colder than his caresses. 'Have I ever suggested it?' When she shook her head nervously, he asked abruptly, 'Well, what makes you think I'm going to suggest it now?'

Gay coloured, but refused to confess that this was something which had occasionally puzzled her. Luke had never pressed his attentions on her as far as this, and she realised he was a very sexy man. He had never asked to become her lover, although the way he had kissed her had hinted that he might like to be. Before she had thought this was because he considered her not good enough for him. Perhaps that was still the reason, she mused unhappily, if in an entirely different way.

'Let's get out of here,' he said brusquely, over an hour later. 'I've had a word with your parents and promised to bring you safely home.'

He sounded cynical, as if he imagined she was more than capable of looking after herself and her parents' concern had privately amused him. Gay sighed as she allowed him to guide her outside and waited while he hailed a taxi. In his present mood she wasn't looking forward to going to his flat, but there didn't seem to be anything she could do about it.

When they reached his flat he removed her wrap and took her to the lounge. The weather was good for May and even at this time of night it was still warm, but he switched on an electric fire. Gay was glad of extra heat, for she was feeling strangely chilled. One moment she seemed burning with fever, the next icy cold.

Luke, after seeing her seated, poured them both a drink. 'Would you rather have coffee?' he asked, as she frowned.

'Not really.' She glanced at him quickly, then away again. She actually felt in need of something stronger than coffee and as she hadn't had much to drink all evening she had few misgivings about accepting whatever it was Luke had given her.

It was merely a dry sherry, which she found reassuring, somehow. At least he wasn't trying to disrupt the clearness of her mind.

'Now,' he began firmly, sitting down opposite, as if he wanted to keep his own mind clear as well, 'I'd like a few answers, Gay, please. Why did you do your best to make a fool of me? You could easily have told me who you were.'

'You didn't want to see me again, so what difference could it have made?' she countered evasively.

He sighed tersely. 'I tried to see you again, the morning after we met in that damned shop. I called at your brother's flat, but it was empty and there was no one to contact. I did ask your friend Jim, but he didn't have a clue.'

Gay looked at him uncertainly. His eyes were narrowed. He looked pale and grim, his mouth set harshly. 'Morris is away,' she mumbled unsteadily, as something in Luke's eyes unnerved her. 'That evening, after I'd seen you in the boutique, I had an urgent message from my mother. She'd sprained her ankle and I had to go to Paris. Morris and I both left early. That's probably how you missed me.'

'It's been like trying to trace a will-o'-the-wisp,' he

muttered, as if to himself.

'Why were you trying to find me?' she whispered, her eyes wide and her voice suddenly hoarse in her throat as she realised what he was saying.

Briefly Luke hesitated. 'One of the reasons was because you looked so ill. You stood in the salon doorway and I thought you were going to pass out. It had to have something to do with me,' he said bluntly.

'You really think so?' she forced a scornful, disbelieving laugh, in a desperate effort to divert him from the truth, 'You have a nerve!'

'You did say you loved me once,' he reminded her ruthlessly, his mouth tightening.

She had to meet this with convincing derision. 'I usually tell all my boy-friends that. Men like to hear it, it makes them feel good, but not many of you are worth loving.'

'So you were merely amusing yourself?' he said savagely.

Gay bit her lip hard to stop it trembling, but he obviously took her silence for a confession of guilt. There was a coldness to his voice as he spoke again.

'Why do your parents let you roam around as you do? You've a good brain. Why don't you use it?'

Her eyes flickered as they met his and fell. 'Not everyone has your ambition, Luke. Is it so wrong for a woman to prefer the simpler things of life? We aren't all the same. Some of us still prefer cooking and housework.'

'Which is fine for those with marriage in mind,' he snapped.

'Well, you hadn't!' Gay flung at him suddenly, from the rather muddled recesses of her brain. The contempt in his eyes made her despairing and reckless. She wasn't sure what she meant herself, and didn't care what he made of it.

His eyes half closed. 'When I first saw a certain girl I had plenty on my mind, including marriage. I thought she was sweet and innocent and I wanted to be the one to teach her things. I soon learnt my mistake.'

'So it wasn't just the lowly position I occupied that put you off,' she said tonelessly, wondering why her heart beat so wildly at the thought of learning from Luke all the things he hinted of.

'Not entirely,' he returned with grim frankness. 'Girls from all walks of life are doing almost anything today. To me it's more important what a girl does with her private life.'

'So she would have to be near perfect before you would consider her for your wife?' Gay cried tauntingly. 'Unless she had other attributes, like Lily Dalmonte, for instance. What happened to her, Luke? Did you aim too high for once? Did she throw you over?'

His face immediately livid, he was on his feet, dragging Gay to hers in seconds. As they stared at each other in terse silence, Gay had a horrid suspicion she had gone too far. Then Luke's hands on her arms were suddenly behind her back, jerking her to him, but the need for his lovemaking so overwhelmed her she didn't fight him. It was so long since she had been in his arms that even though they were hard and hurting she welcomed the fact that they were around her.

When his mouth descended harshly on her own she groaned weakly. They kissed passionately, her arms curving around his neck, trying to hold him as fiercely as he held her. There was no room for tenderness in either of their minds, only a silent, desperate communication of straining bodies and lips.

As she began shuddering helplessly, Luke lifted his head to say roughly, 'You needed that as much as I did, Gay.'

She stared at him, her eyelids heavy, her body swept by sensations she no longer knew how to cope with. Bitterly she nodded, her lips twisting in the humiliating knowledge that she couldn't deny it. Or him. Whatever Luke asked of her she might be too weak to refuse.

He was saying, his arms still tight around her, 'If you must know about Lily, we don't see each other any more. You could say the decision was hers.'

Gay frowned, wondering if this were true. Her eyes stared into his, but all she saw was cool, determined mockery. Was it for himself or Lily? Perhaps she would never know.

While she considered, she felt his hand gently brushing back her tumbled hair. 'I'm still attracted to a girl I once picked up in a strange town,' he said softly, his glance teasing, then very sober. 'Would you marry me, Gay?'

'Marry you?' A few weeks ago she might have accepted eagerly, but tonight his cold-blooded proposal left her horrified. The warmth she had felt in his arms changed into anger and she tried to draw away from him.

He wouldn't let her go but spoke her name urgently when she froze like a statue. Fighting against shock, she drew a deep breath and tried to look him straight in the face. Fleetingly she was tempted to say yes and make his life hell. The moment passed, however, as common sense took its place.

'You've left it a bit late,' she exclaimed. 'You don't respect me, Luke, and that hasn't changed, even if, in your eyes, my social position has.'

'I'm asking you to marry me. Your social position doesn't matter,' he said steadily.

'Doesn't it?' Her eyes widened scornfully. 'You can't expect me to believe that when you told me yourself you intended to marry well.'

'Perhaps I changed my mind before I learnt about your father,' he retorted, his mouth tightening impatiently.

'You might change it again,' she cried, 'if you knew his title isn't hereditary. He was only awarded it because of work which he's done. We have no blue blood in our veins, and very little money.'

'For God's sake shut up, Gay,' he said tersely. 'I know all about your father. I've actually known him for years, on a business footing.'

'That must be why I've never met you,' she said bleakly. 'Daddy knows so many people, he couldn't possibly invite them all home.'

'I've met your mother before,' he conceded, 'but not your brother. When you disappeared I tried to trace you through him, but no one seemed to have heard of a photographer named Fenton.'

'Morris is my half-brother,' Gay explained flatly. 'His own mother died when he was ten, but he still remembers her. When he started up on his own he used her name. Actually it was my mother, his stepmother, who suggested it, when he didn't want to use Fenton.'

'How do he and your mother get on?' Luke asked.

'Very well,' Gay replied briefly. 'They always have.'

'You'd better not mention that I thought him a rather disreputable character,' Luke said grimly. 'I'm afraid I was prejudiced on your behalf. I thought he wasn't looking after you properly.'

'You thought he was my boy-friend,' she reminded him coldly.

'I was ready to be jealous of any man who came near you. I still am,' he warned, his eyes hardening.

Gay said quickly, suddenly frightened because he sounded so threatening, 'Morris left on a job, the same day as I went to Paris, as I told you, but he married Julie, his girl-friend, while they were in South Africa and they're still there, honeymooning.'

'As we could be doing,' Luke said smoothly, 'just as soon as you agree to marrying me.'

Gay was aware of her stomach muscles tightening at the mere thought of spending a honeymoon with Luke. Again she tried to wrench free of him, but was only pulled closer. As if to punish her for it, his mouth moved nearer.

'It's crazy to be standing here arguing like this,' she

gasped, beginning to struggle in earnest.

'It's no use trying to fight me,' he said roughly. 'We can stand here all night, if necessary, until you say yes.'

He began kissing her again, as if he had a good idea what his kisses did to her, and now there was a ruthless quality to his caresses to which her body began responding alarmingly.

'I want you,' he muttered thickly, against her vulnerable mouth, 'I've wanted you for a long time. I can hardly keep my hands off you. You'd better give in, Gay.'

How could she? As his hands and lips transported her to a wonderful dream world, she made a final effort to hold on to her sanity. Luke didn't love her, she told herself desperately. He would only marry her because he needed a wife. Since Lily Dalmonte had turned him down, he probably considered Gay Fenton the next best thing. And his nerve was so cool it enabled him to forget that, until this evening, he hadn't been at all keen even to be seen taking her out for a drink!

Yet as always, when she was driven to defying him outright, a sense of caution held her back. There was still the complication of David and Katrina, which now seemed so silly, but which would no doubt throw Luke into a fury of contempt, should he learn the truth of it.

If she did agree to do as he asked, what would marriage with him be like? Wouldn't it merely bring her fresh misery, feeling as she did about him? Panic-stricken, as she felt her slim body clinging to him, she tried to think of a convincing excuse.

'Luke,' averting her flushed face, she murmured breathlessly, 'I can't marry you because I'm thinking of marrying Nigel.'

'Trent?'

Unsteadily, as he abruptly released her, she nodded. 'He's asked me.'

'And you refused him?' Luke's eyes narrowed as he caught a hint of her uncertainty.

'I'm considering it.' Gay swallowed, her eyes veiled.

'Can he make you feel as I do?' Luke asked, suddenly violent. 'When I kiss you, you tremble, and I don't think it's from fear. What sort of relationship do you have with Trent, exactly?' he sneered, with sarcastic mockery. As she stared at him helplessly, he advised tersely, 'You'd better decide not to marry him, Gay, just as fast as you can.'

'Which doesn't mean I'd agree to marrying you!' she cried, raising her head to glare at him defiantly. 'It must be a joke that you should even think of asking me after—after everything, but at least you can't force me to agree.'

'Listen to me, Gay,' his hands descended on her shoulders, shaking her lightly, as if he was trying to get through to a particularly dense child. 'Have you considered my proposition from every angle? Wouldn't being the wife of a leading industrialist give you something to do, if nothing else? I may not be out of the top drawer,' he observed dryly, 'but I have enough money, with which you can amuse yourself. If you like working,' his voice became even drier, 'you can begin on my country house right away. My aunt's gone back to her cottage, so you can have a free hand. As long as you keep your evenings free for me.' His hands cupped her cheeks, turning her face up to him. 'I should want to love you far into the night,' he said huskily.

'No!' Gay almost choked as her breath caught in her throat at such a prospect. Didn't he know what a suggestion like that did to her?

Luke stared down coldly at her hot face. 'I'd try changing that to yes, if I were you,' he snapped.

'Is—is that a threat?'

'No,' he exclaimed curtly. 'I may have used threats to get you here, but I won't use blackmail to get a wife. Just let me say,' he added remorselessly, 'that a lot of men wouldn't have you, I'm sure the self-righteous Mr Trent included, if they knew as much about you as I do.'

'Why, you . . .!' As a swift rage consumed Gay, she tried to slap his hard cheek.

'No, you don't!' he snapped between his teeth, catching her hand.

They stared at each other, in a kind of grim impasse. 'It may take time,' he assured her, 'but I usually get what I want in the end.'

'But I don't love you!' she gulped, flinching from such absolute ruthlessness.

His eyes darkened, smouldering. 'So I realise, but whatever it is that turns you on whenever I touch you, I'll settle for it.'

His eyes were running over her, his gaze insolent, as if he meant to shock her. She shivered as his words evoked a strange kind of fear. 'You have no right to say such things!' she protested.

His mouth curved in a sardonic smile. 'I fully intend to have every right—and soon. For a start, you can see Trent tomorrow and tell him you won't be seeing him again. Perhaps,' he drawled coolly, 'all things considered, I can afford to be generous.'

Gay longed to defy him, but was suddenly afraid. He had only to take her in his arms again and she might find herself agreeing to anything. Luke said no more threats, but she wasn't sure she could trust him. He was hard, she didn't know how he would react if completely thwarted. It might pay her to be devious.

'If you like. Nigel did ask me to have dinner with him, tomorrow evening,' she said, which was true, 'but I can't promise that he'll listen to me.'

'We'll see,' Luke replied enigmatically. 'Come,' he took her arm, with the air of a man biding his time, 'I'll take you home and see you the day after tomorrow. That should give you long enough to get yourself sorted out and get rid of Trent.'

Gay spent the rest of the night, what was left of it, thinking. She couldn't sleep and gave up trying, and the morning found her listless and heavy-eyed.

At breakfast her mother frowned at the sight of her. 'You're looking tired this morning, darling. I hope Luke Ashley didn't upset you?'

'No more than usual,' Gay retorted, then regretted answering so unwisely. Unwittingly she had aroused her mother's curiosity.

'How well do you know him?' Patricia cast a sharper glance at her daughter's pale face. 'Actually, I didn't know you'd even met him.'

'It was a while ago,' Gay disclosed reluctantly, recalling Nigel asking much the same thing. 'We've been out together a few times.'

'When he told your father and me he was taking you out last night, I fancied he was worried about something,' Patricia mused lightly. 'Of course it might have had nothing to do with you, but it seemed to me he was a man with a problem.'

Gay flushed and said sharply, 'I'm sure there won't be much that he can't solve.'

Patricia frowned. 'I merely wondered.'

'You must,' Gay was still sharp, 'have better things to think about.'

'Well,' her mother laughed rather ruefully, 'he is the kind of man women tend to dream about. Someone was saying at the reception that there's a rumour going round that he might be going to marry Lily Dalmonte. Do you know if it's true?'

'I don't think so, but you never know.' Gay felt sick and changed the subject abruptly: 'Would you mind if I went to Wales?'

'Whatever for?' Patricia exclaimed, looking completely astonished. 'You've only just got back from Paris.'

They had a small cottage in Wales, which Gay's father had bought for a song twenty years ago. It was still too remote to be worth a lot, but he and Patricia loved it as a retreat when their busy life occasionally got too much for them.

'I think I'd like a few days there, on my own,' Gay glanced at her mother rather desperately. 'There doesn't have to be a special reason, does there?'

'No, of course not . . .'

Gay rushed on. 'I have to think seriously about my future and I don't seem able to do that here.'

'No, perhaps not.' Patricia stared at her daughter, her brow furrowed anxiously. 'We haven't been to the cottage for months and it must need airing, so it might be a good idea if you did go. Your father and I don't think we can manage to get there before the end of June.'

'Then you won't mind?'

'Would you take any notice if I did?' Patricia asked wryly. 'You like your own way, Gay, and your father spoils you.'

Gay digested this in silence. Was it true? She tried to be a good daughter, but perhaps she didn't always succeed. 'I'm sorry,' she began anxiously, for she loved her parents very much and would never deliberately cause either one of them pain.

'Oh, I didn't mean to sound critical, darling,' Patricia cut her short with a penitent smile. 'As a daughter you're marvellous. I was actually trying to consider you from a man's point of view. I was wondering if you were perhaps running away because of Nigel. I know he doesn't find you easy to manage, and you never seem to have much patience with him.'

'Don't I?' Gay had never meant to give this impression, certainly not in front of her mother.

'I've told him you need a strong hand.'

'Well, thank you very much!' Gay exclaimed indignantly, then, more calmly, 'I'm sorry, Mums, but I don't love Nigel, so it would be lunacy to marry him. I've already told him—and he isn't the reason why I'm going to Wales.'

'It doesn't have anything to do with Luke Ashley, by any chance?' Patricia asked suddenly.

About to deny it, Gay changed her mind. Her mother was too shrewd to be fooled easily. 'Not really,' she replied flatly, deciding that a sprinkling of truth might be more convincing than outright denial. 'We've had a difference of opinion, a slight quarrel, I suppose, but that's all.'

'I—er—see ...' said Patricia, so obviously full of curiosity that Gay felt a reluctant admiration for her when she merely nodded and rose to her feet. 'Well,' she shrugged, 'if you're really set on Wales I'd better go and pack you some provisions. Meanwhile, you could always give your father a ring and tell him where you're off to.'

CHAPTER SEVEN

WHEN Gay reached the cottage that evening she was conscious of a great feeling of relief. All day she had been frightened that something or someone would stop her from reaching her destination. When nothing did she found it difficult to believe in her good fortune.

She had borrowed her mother's small car, which was seldom used in town, and hoped that the springs hadn't suffered over the last three miles of rough road. The cottage was isolated, surrounded by mountains, but the area was so beautiful she rarely noticed the lack of amenities.

After breakfast, she had been in such a hurry to get away, she hadn't done anything other than ring Nigel to cancel their dinner date. After her refusing to marry him, Nigel didn't seem surprised that she no longer wanted to dine with him, but she had flinched as she had sensed his disappointment. Sometimes she wondered if she was too softhearted, as she hated hurting anyone.

She had packed quickly, taking only a few casual clothes. There were heavy boots and outdoor coats at the cottage, so she didn't have to bother bringing these. Her mother had packed a huge box of provisions—more, Gay was sure, than she would ever need. The provisions and loan of the car, Patricia declared, could be considered part payment for the work Gay had done in Paris. Whatever the reason, Gay felt grateful.

She might even have enjoyed her rushed preparations as she loved the cottage, if she hadn't expected every minute to be interrupted by Luke. On leaving London she had had a terrible fear of being pursued by him, a fear that had strangely given way to disappointment when not once during her journey had there been any sign of him. He probably wouldn't give her another thought, Gay decided bitterly, once he realised she was gone.

The setting sun outlined the mountain tops with gold as she drew up outside the door, causing a small gasp of pleasure to escape her lips and make her glad she had come. The cottage, too, seemed to welcome her. As a house it wasn't large, but Patricia had always taken a lot of trouble over it and it was cosy and comfortable.

The huge brick fireplace in the lounge was already laid with dry logs and soon Gay had a warm fire going. She had been taught how to look after herself and do such things by parents who believed their children should at least learn to be practical. After building up the fire she threw open the windows. Even an hour or two before bedtime might remove the faintly musty smell from the rooms, the direct result of being closed up. Before she went to bed, she reminded herself, she must remember to close them again.

It wasn't until much later, when she stood at the door, before bolting it for the night, that she allowed herself to think of Luke. It was pleasant to linger in her dressing-gown, breathing in the sweet Welsh air and she resented that he crept into her thoughts unawares. Why couldn't she keep him out? It must be crazy, when she was doing her uttermost to forget him, that she should think of him continually.

Something fell on her cheek and she frowned with surprise to find it was a tear. Impatiently she rubbed it away and tried to concentrate on something else. In the end she gave in to her clamouring senses which wouldn't let her, and concentrated instead on all the reasons why she shouldn't love Luke.

He had been attracted, obviously still was, but because he had thought her just an ordinary girl he had put her firmly out of his life. Then, when his urgent pursuit of a rich Society girl failed and he had discovered that the Fentons, if not actually aristocrats, were socially acceptable, he had changed his mind and decided Gay might just be good enough. The more Gay thought of it—the way in which he arrogantly expected to be able to walk back into her life without a word of reproach—brought fury as well as tears to her eyes. She'd be a fool to have anything more to do with him, she assured herself, and because of this was convinced that coming here was the most sensible thing she could have done.

Yet, for all she imagined she had got everything sorted out, she didn't sleep well, and the next morning found her as unrefreshed as she had been the previous morning. And while it was easy enough to blame the strangeness of her bed, it was the bed she had slept in on holiday for years, so this excuse didn't seem altogether feasible. It would be nearer the truth, she supposed, to admit that Luke had something to do with it. Luke and the isolation of the cottage. Throughout the night the wind had howled around the chimneys and the creaking of old timbers had made her both restless and nervous.

Well, she would have to get used to it. It was a bit late now to remember she hadn't been to the cottage on her own before. Gay shrugged her slender shoulders as she scrambled down the last incline of the crag she had climbed to walk back home. The air today was still wonderful. She had been abroad many times with her parents, but she loved Wales and didn't think there were many places to equal it. The people, too, were pleasant and kind. It would be no great hardship to spend a week or two here, even if the wind did howl in the night and she had no company.

For dinner that evening she cooked the chicken her mother had insisted on including in her provisions.

'You can resort to tins later, Gay,' she had advised. As the larder of the cottage didn't get any sun it was as good as an ice-box, so what Gay didn't manage to get through tonight would keep.

Unfortunately she allowed a sudden longing for something hot to distort her judgement, and she was frowning with dismay at the subsequent spread when there came a brief knock on the kitchen door and Luke walked through it.

Gay stared at him with something approaching horror in her eyes. He was wearing a pair of old but spotless jeans which fitted his muscular thighs to perfection. With them he wore a dark shirt, open at the neck and, over this, a slightly heavier jacket. His dark hair was ruffled, as if he had been walking in the wind, but it was the sheer masculine vitality in his face that struck her like a blow. A curious little light flickered like a flame in his eyes as he studied her. This alone, apart from his powerful build, was enough to warn her that here was no weakling she could easily cope with. Instinctively he reminded her of the mountains outside, hard and strong and, to the transgressor, unforgiving.

She drew in a huge measure of much needed breath and inhaled quickly. 'W—what on earth are you doing here?' she stammered, her face growing pale as the full implications of his sudden appearance began hitting her, and the fright she had received on first seeing him gave way to fear of a different kind. His eyes, she noticed, still smouldered with anger.

He gave a short laugh. 'Why shouldn't I be here? I'm your fiancé, aren't I?'

'You must be out of your mind!' she gasped, staring at him defiantly. 'There was nothing definite.'

'As good as—and you know it.' He dropped the rucksack he was carrying from his broad shoulders to the floor. 'If you don't enjoy seeing me, then let me assure you I haven't particularly enjoyed having to chase half way over the country to find you. I happened to have a conference this afternoon which wasn't easy to cancel. If it hadn't been for that I would have been here sooner.'

Gay's eyes widened and she felt her own anger rising. 'Who told you where to find me?' she asked.

'I rang this morning to confirm our date this evening, only to hear you were gone. I spoke to your mother.'

'But she wouldn't tell you where I was.'

'Oh, yes, she did,' he spoke between his teeth, 'after I went to see her and told her I was going to marry her daughter. And in the near future,' he added grimly, 'no longer than a week or two, at the most, after we return to London.'

'You're crazy!' she gasped, feeling completely betrayed. 'My mother promised not to tell anyone.'

'You could hardly expect her not to, in the circumstances,' he snapped.

'And she believed you?' Gay felt incredulous.

'She's woman enough to believe in a lovers' quarrel,' Luke said cynically. 'She was also worried about you being here on your own.'

'I wanted to be here on my own!' Gay found herself almost shouting, scarcely realising what she was saying. 'Can't you get that into your thick head!'

The fury in his face was momentarily frightening. She shrank back, thinking he was about to slap her, but he contented himself with seizing her shoulders in a vice-like grip. 'Don't ever speak to me like that again,' he breathed, his nostrils white.

'I—I don't care,' she muttered sullenly, biting her lip.

'You'll care all right,' he retorted harshly, thrusting her quickly away, as if not trusting himself to hold her any longer.

The threat in his voice affected her breathing so that she had to take a few deep breaths before she could go on. 'How did you get here?' she panted, rubbing her sore shoulder, the angry reproach in her eyes meant to convey how much he had hurt her.

'By car,' he replied abruptly.

'I didn't hear one. Did you leave it by the ford?'

'I left it,' he named the nearest town, 'in a garage there for a week or so. Then I took a taxi for part of the way and the last few miles I walked. I thought that was the best idea as your mother warned me about the ford.'

'I wish you'd drowned in it!' she cried bitterly, thinking of the river practically outside the door.

'I'm sure you do,' he replied curtly, his voice cold, while his expression warned her again to be careful of what she said.

'You would soon become bored in a place like this,' she flung at him tensely, wishing he would go.

He shrugged, a little of his anger dissolving in flinty amusement. 'The pleasure of taming you, my dear girl, might add a little spice to dull days.'

'You're despicable!' she trembled, her blue eyes darkening.

Luke merely shook his head, a pitying gesture that made her want to scream. 'You like to think so,' he mocked.

They stared at each other until Gay grew confused and her mouth went dry. 'If you had to come,' she said at last, as the silence between them became more than she could bear, 'you should have waited until tomorrow. It's almost dark.'

Briefly his glance went to the laden stove behind her. 'I couldn't have picked a better time, if you ask me. That smells good.'

She turned her glossy head dazedly to follow his eyes and comprehend his meaning. 'You can't have my food,' she snapped, feeling as taut as a bowstring. 'I need all I have. I can't replace it, you know. There isn't a supermarket on the doorstep!'

'Gay!' he broke in, his black brows lifting. 'How many times do I have to tell you, you talk too much. I expect, right now, it's because of the isolation.'

His taunting remark didn't make her feel better. She

flushed and exclaimed angrily, 'I think you've got a nerve to invite yourself here, when you must know you aren't wanted! And not only do you walk in without warning, but you begin insulting me without even taking the time to—to say hello!'

'I'm sorry,' he apologised, but with no genuine hint of remorse. His eyes flicking contemptuously over her, he reached her side and, before she could move, dropped a swift, hard kiss on her startled lips. 'Was this what you missed?' he asked, coldly audacious. 'Should I do it again, just for good measure? I don't like to feel I'm depriving you of anything.'

She tried to push him away, but wasn't quick enough to prevent a further assault. This time his arms went around her as if he was determined she should have no room for complaint. His head lowered, he kissed her soft mouth, forcing her lips apart without mercy, holding her so tightly she could have cried out with pain. Yet even while she struggled, Gay was disconcerted to find electric sparks piercing the skin of her cheeks and flicking through her body.

When he eventually released her she was creamy pale, her brow faintly beaded with perspiration. 'You're impossible—and hateful!' she blazed, jerking back to put a safer yard or two between them. Every part of her felt shaken by the insistence of his cruel mouth, and she knew she had to get rid of him. With dismay her glance fell on the rucksack at his feet. It seemed to suggest he expected not only a meal but to be staying.

'You can't stay!' she whispered hoarsely, her throat constricted. 'Anyway, I've come here for peace and quiet.'

'So have I,' he mocked, regarding her with a trace of ironic amusement. 'And, of course, you. Although whether I acquire any of these three things remains to be seen. Certainly the welcome I've received, so far, leaves me in considerable doubt.'

'You have no rights . . .' she began indignantly, but firmly he held up a hand.

'Gay, please! I'm hungry. I've been travelling for hours and haven't stopped for a meal. We can go into the question of rights, etcetera, after supper, if you insist. I certainly might feel more like dealing with your foolish accusations after I've been fed.'

Gay refused to believe there was a hint of softer amusement in his eyes, or that she might be weakening.

'No!' she cried fiercely, 'I won't give you anything. If you refuse to go then you'll have to help yourself!' Pushing past him wildly, she fled from the small kitchen up the stairs.

He caught her as she reached the top, spinning her around to face his renewed impatience. There was anger now in his eyes, as his glance leapt over her, taking in the pink flush of colour underlying her creamy pale skin. 'If you didn't look so absolutely breakable, I think I'd be tempted to beat you,' he said tersely.

Her head tilted back as she stared at him. Such intensity terrified yet excited her and she felt herself tremble. Luke's grey eyes, roaming sensuously over her body, darkened compellingly and she gazed at him as though mesmerised. The nervous flare of her delicate nostrils softened the restraint she had put on her mouth so that it curved, suddenly, wilfully.

'I wish you hadn't come,' she said huskily, as if almost ready to admit her own vulnerability.

'Why not ask me why?' he challenged, throwing an obvious restraint on himself.

'No . . .' She wasn't prepared to listen to something she wasn't ready for. The touch of his hand was intolerable. He still held her arm and the restless grip of his fingers burned right through her. Some strange heat from them seemed to be searing both her body and mind. The atmosphere between them was brittle with tension and suddenly desperate to get away from him, she gave in.

'All right,' she exclaimed, 'I'll give you your supper, if you promise not to touch me.'

His eyes glinted, the silver very clear and glittery as they searched her face. 'Now why should that scare you, I wonder?'

'Couldn't you give me a straight answer, just this once?' she pleaded, a funny little pulse she couldn't see beating in her throat, clearly visible to the man.

'No,' he replied harshly, his mouth set in a hard line, 'nor will I make promises I might not be able to keep.'

Why was he so implacable? 'I don't want you touching me because I hate you!' she whispered vehemently, putting everything she had into sounding convincing. She would never tell him that when he held her ecstasy flooded her body until she was unable to even think straight.

His eyes suddenly sparkling with ill humour, Luke retorted smoothly, 'That's challenge enough for any man, my child, and one I fully intend taking up. You might be thankful that at the moment I'm allowing my hunger for food to subdue my other appetites.'

Gay's breath caught painfully. 'You don't care what you say to me, do you?'

He laughed with little humour. 'If you mean do I occasionally enjoy shocking you, then the answer has to be yes. For all your permissiveness, I doubt if any of your previous boy-friends have managed to teach you much. I'm more than willing to wager you could learn a lot from me—which you'd never forget.'

Her eyes flashed with a mixture of hurt and indignant fury. 'Did you come here just to threaten?'

His eyes lit with a latent mockery, and something else. 'So you consider me a laggard for not suiting actions to words?' he drawled. And when she glanced at him blankly, he stunned her by lifting her softly rounded chin to drop another hard kiss on her mouth.

As a quick, answering passion rushed through her, she jerked back. Her pale cheeks flaming, she fumed, 'You—you twist everything I say, don't you, to serve your own ends?'

'It gets easier with practice,' he taunted. Then, as she gritted her small white teeth, he grinned, 'Come on, my small spitfire, let's stop arguing for five minutes and eat. It must be your red hair that makes you so disagreeable.'

Shooting him another outraged glance, Gay escaped, when he let her go, to the kitchen. Here she served the chicken, mercifully still hot and succulent, while Luke leant against the wall by the cooker and watched her.

'No duck tonight?' he drawled.

Refusing to be drawn, she ignored him, although her heartbeats increased when he reminded her of the first time she had met him. Continuing with what she was doing, she was surprised she didn't make any mistakes. She found concentration increasingly difficult as she also remembered Luke thought her permissive. By telling him the truth she could make him apologise about that. Wouldn't it be nice to see him having to eat his words as well as his dinner?

She opened a tin of peas and made some gravy. She hadn't been going to bother with gravy just for herself, but she knew Luke liked it. While she put the prepared vegetables in their serving dishes, he removed his jacket and went upstairs to wash, after asking where he might find the bathroom.

When he came down again, he took the hot dishes from her and carried them to the table. 'You're a very good cook,' he admired her efforts appreciatively, 'I can see I'm going to be well looked after.'

Glancing at him uneasily, Gay gave him the chicken to carve—a task, she was forced to admit, if grudgingly, he did admirably. She had thought he would have been too busy expanding his business empire to have remembered, or even learnt, how to do such things.

Dinner was a curiously silent meal, and although Gay ate sparingly, Luke, she noticed, piled his plate twice.

'Are you sure you've had enough?' she enquired sarcastically, resenting his apparent ability to enjoy his food while she could do scarcely more than nibble.

With a satisfied sigh he pushed his plate aside. 'It seemed a shame to waste it,' he replied mildly, 'Why did you make so much?'

'I'm not sure,' she muttered, glancing away from his dark face and the look of faint enquiry in his eyes. 'I suppose I wasn't thinking what I was doing.'

'Why not?' He studied her hot cheeks intently.

'I don't have to answer everything!' She began gathering up their empty plates, 'I'm sorry there's no pudding.'

'I'd just as soon have coffee, if it's available.'

'It's ready.' Reaching for it, she hesitated. 'But shouldn't you be going?'

'Where?'

'Please!' Leaving the coffee on the tray, she stumbled to the sink, running cold water over the dishes with unnecessary force. 'Do I have to explain everything? You must know what I mean.'

'Not really.' Firmly he turned off the tap and removed her from the sink. 'I have no intention of seeking alternative accommodation, if that's what you mean.'

'It is!' she hissed, wondering wildly how she was going to get rid of him. He looked about as removable as a chunk of rock!

Coolly Luke shook his dark head. 'Nothing doing, I'm afraid. And, before you get even more hot and bothered, why don't we go to the lounge and talk?'

Meeting his eyes, Gay looked away hastily. 'We did that two nights ago. We can't have anything left to say to each other.'

His mouth tightened at her stubborn refusal to accept the situation. 'I have plenty,' he retorted, 'and I'm sure you'll think of something.'

Clenching her hands tightly. Gay frowned at his cynicism, but he refused to be diverted. Picking up the coffee tray, he guided her firmly from the kitchen. 'The lounge?' he enquired grimly, pausing in the hall.

Unable to fight him any longer, Gay led the way while he followed.

'Ah, this is nice!' Placing the tray he carried on a small table, Luke glanced around with undisguised interest. 'Too often a weekend cottage is too basic for my liking. Who's responsible?'

Gay sat down with a resigned sigh. 'My mother. She's good at this sort of thing. Before she married Daddy she was an interior designer. She still likes doing up houses. Nowadays, though, she only helps friends.'

'What about you?' Luke turned his attention on Gay again. 'Have you inherited any of your mother's talent? Are you ready to make a start on the houses I own?'

Recalling the faultless decor of his flat, she doubted if anyone could improve on it. Forgetting she had declared that she had nothing to say, she began with a rush. 'I know nothing about the houses you own, Luke, nor do I intend to. You had no right to tell my parents that we're engaged and when we—I mean you return to London, you'll just have to go and tell them we're not! And it's your own fault if it causes you some embarrassment.'

'If you insist,' he replied sardonically, sitting himself beside her and stretching his long legs to the fire. 'My discomfort might be nothing to yours, though. Not after spending a week here with me.'

Gay glared at him, not relishing this unpalatable truth. 'I won't spend a day here with you,' she said, adding fretfully, 'I still can't understand why my mother told you where I was.'

'Maybe she approves of me as a prospective son-in-law and believes we all have a right to look after our own.'

'You don't own me yet! And,' she snapped, somewhat irrationally, 'if all you can do is run to my mother behind my back, then you never will.'

Luke merely raised indifferent brows and said mildly, 'At least I've never tried to deceive you.'

'Meaning,' Gay frowned, after a short pause, 'that's what I've been doing—trying to deceive you?'

'You went off without telling me,' he reminded her dryly. 'If one of my staff had so transgressed, I'd have fired them immediately.'

'Just because they didn't let you know where they were going?' she asked incredulously.

'Hardly,' he snapped. 'I'm talking generally, about deception.'

'Oh, I see.' Gay stirred uneasily. Luke's words brought back the problem of David and Katrina. She again toyed with the idea of telling him the truth about them, but as always she found herself hesitating. Such a confession could bring problems for David, and would it really matter whether Luke knew or not? Her pulse might race madly every time he was near her, but, after Lily Dalmonte, she knew he would never love her. So what future could they have together, despite everything he said to the contrary?

In coming here this evening he had probably meant to force her to give in to his demands. But, if he insisted on staying, she must leave, perhaps after he was in bed. Her car was at the door and she was familiar with the countryside, even in the dark. It ought to be quite easy to escape, if she used her brains.

Trying to use them now, she smiled at him uncertainly, as though conceding he had a point. 'I'm sorry, Luke.'

'Famous last words!' he muttered wryly, yet seemed willing enough to accept her apology, if his eyes were faintly sceptical as they rested on her suddenly pleading face.

'I—I've said I'm sorry,' she allowed the uncertainty in her eyes to deepen innocently. 'What more can I say?'

'Nothing, for the moment.' He smiled suddenly, almost tenderly, and drew her unexpectedly to him.

Gay's first instinct, as always, was to fight him, but she realised in time that this wouldn't help to convince him of her change of mind. And, as his head dropped and the light pressure of his mouth on her own made her quiver, she doubted if she really wanted to fight him at all.

'You're beautiful.' His mouth left hers briefly to touch her cheek while his roving hands slipped inside her pants to release her shirt, so he might caress the smooth softness of her back. 'Beautiful,' he murmered huskily.

Her traitorous heart beat violently, but it was only when he turned her completely into his arms and began kissing her forcefully that she stirred uneasily. He crushed her mouth with deep, drugging kisses, demanding and receiving an increasing response. He aroused in her the wild sensations she had known with him before, and her senses were reeling as his hands came round to explore her firm young breasts. Then his breath was rasping in his throat, his desire no longer gentle.

Thrusting her back on the settee, he came down beside her. Here they lay panting, entangled, consumed by an overwhelming mutual passion. Gay could feel his stomach muscles contracting as he felt her trembling under him, and he fought against the powerful need of immediate possession.

'I want you, Gay,' he groaned thickly, 'and I don't know what I'm going to do about it!'

The uncertainty in his voice proved her undoing. She had never heard him evenly remotely unsure of himself before, and suddenly all she desired was to please him. As his mouth sought hers in mounting hunger, her arms reached up to encircle his neck, and, as their lips clung endlessly, all sense of caution fled. She was beyond protest, only conscious of Luke and the feverish pressures of their mounting desire for each other. As the warm wash of sensual feeling flooded her, sweeping her swiftly into deep, uncharted waters, she became weakly submissive, unable to deny him anything.

Her eyes closed tightly, as the pleasure she was experiencing became so intense it made her dizzy. Luke continued to caress her throbbing body, but now his movements were jerky, as though he was trying to hang on to the last of his self-control.

Later, Gay was ashamed that she made no effort to help him. She loved Luke and, because of this, only wanted to placate and satisfy him. The time she had known him might have been short, but the love she felt for him, she suspected, had nothing to do with time. For no other man had she ever felt such a tremendous reaching out inside herself and she knew a great yearning to make him content. The furnace of desire burning inside her, along with a seemingly natural ability to respond exactly to his every movement, assured her hazily that she could do this quite easily. And, although she dimly recognised it was wrong, she appeared to have lost all power to resist him. Her wilful body arched under his, until his hard virility began hurting and she whimpered mindlessly against his lips.

It was Luke who eventually applied the brakes, changing everything abruptly. Wrenching Gay's arms from around his neck, he cursed harshly under his breath as he rolled away from her. Retreating to the other end of the settee, he smoothed an unsteady hand over his dark hair. His voice was rough and filled with self-derision as he muttered something about their coffee getting cold.

As he poured it out, while she tried to compose herself, he apologised grimly, 'I'm sorry, Gay. I hope you don't feel too let down.'

A chill sensation cooling her skin, she stared at him uncomprehendingly. She ought to be thankful that he had let her go while the passion between them had still been controllable, but her gratitude was, inexplicably, less than her shameful disappointment.

'Why should I feel let down?' she muttered sullenly. 'I know you don't love me.'

'That has nothing to do with it,' he replied tersely.

Gay raised her eyes to look at him, hurt making her suddenly unmindful of what she said. 'I suppose you make love to so many women that it's easy to reject one occasionally.'

'I haven't been able to want another woman since I met you, Gay,' he returned tightly, his eyes cold with hostility as they rested on her, as though he secretly resented such a state of affairs.

'What about Miss Dalmonte?' she accused, disbelievingly.

'I've told you, Gay,' he snapped, 'I don't want to talk about her. Listen to me,' he sighed impatiently, 'I came here, my dear girl, so we could get to know each other better. I want to make love to you, but not this way. I hope you understand?'

A strange sense of bleakness passed over her. Luke wanted to make love to her, but he didn't love her. While she had been on fire with longing in his embrace she had known it wasn't merely a desire to belong to him physically. If he had loved her she could willingly have shared his life, not just his bed, although that, she knew instinctively, would be very important to both of them.

When at last she managed a careless nod, he stared at her pale face. He appeared slightly puzzled, but eventually turned away to pass her coffee. Obediently Gay took it, swallowing it submissively, as if understanding and agreeing with everything he said. Effectively she hid the pain in her heart as, more than ever, she realised the importance of getting away from him. It amused Luke to talk in riddles, but if he had her in his arms again, he might not be able to stop. And the love she felt for him would be no weapon to fight him with. Only by appearing reconciled to his staying, however, might she successfully deaden his suspicions and still make her escape.

After finishing her coffee she got quickly to her feet, saying she was going to bed. 'I'm tired, Luke. I hope you don't mind.'

'I don't mind at all,' he assured her curtly, almost as if he welcomed the prospect of being relieved of her disturbing presence. 'You might show me where I'm to sleep, though, before you go. If it's not too much trouble.'

'I'll show you,' she replied meekly, her eyes lowered as she made for the stairs. As they climbed them, a torrent of rain spattered the front door. 'The weather seems to be changing,' she remarked coolly. 'Aren't you afraid you'll be bored?'

'Not with you,' he replied, so cynically that she wasn't sure if it was a compliment.

She showed him into the spare room. There were four bedrooms in the cottage, although none of them were large. This one had a huge double bed and she hoped Luke would be so comfortable he wouldn't stir. If he had had a busy day, as well as walking all the distance from the main road, there was every likelihood that he would sleep soundly.

'I think I may as well turn in, too,' he said, flexing his broad shoulders. 'I see you have a shower in the bathroom. Would you mind if I used it?'

'Not at all,' she answered dryly, 'make yourself at home. Goodnight.'

'Goodnight, Gay,' he returned politely, waiting for her to leave him. As she hesitated, gazing at him nervously, he snapped harshly. 'For heaven's sake, Gay, what is it now? I thought you were in a hurry to get to bed.'

Feeling herself tremble, Gay bit her lip, fighting against an irrational desire to throw herself in his arms. What a fool she was! Would she never learn? Downstairs, Luke had clearly rejected her. 'It was nothing,' she answered bleakly, 'nothing at all.'

His mouth tight, Luke stared at her briefly, then, his jaw clamped tersely, he turned without another word and left her.

As his bedroom door closed behind him sharply, she stared at it for a long, apprehensive moment. It was no good tormenting herself wishing for things she couldn't have. In a few hours she would be leaving Luke for ever. And while he might be furious when he first discovered she was gone, he might eventually enjoy the cottage better without her.

CHAPTER EIGHT

In her room, Gay closed the door and carefully penned a brief note for Luke. In it she assured him he was welcome to use the cottage for as long as he liked, but that she couldn't possibly stay, now he was here. She didn't say she wouldn't be seeing him again, but she hoped, ironically, that he could read between the lines.

Sitting on the edge of her bed while waiting for Luke to retire, she thought of what had just taken place between them in the lounge. She felt ashamed of the part she had played, but even more bewildered by his attitude. He had wanted to make love to her and while she was increasingly grateful that he had controlled himself in time, she also felt curious about it. On one or two occasions now, when, Gay flushed to admit, she had been over-responsive, he had held back. He was a man, she felt sure, not used to denying himself, which made his restraint with her all the more puzzling. The explanation would have been easy if he had respected her, but he had told her so many times that he did not that this couldn't be the answer.

If only she could stop remembering! If only the pain hadn't been intense enough to make her want to cry out. She dreaded leaving him, but stronger than that was her fear of staying and having him discover how much she cared for him. Yet, two hours later, it took every scrap of willpower she could find to enable her to pick up her suitcase and steal quietly from the house.

It was still raining, and she shivered as the wind blew a heavy shower directly in her face. Uneasily she peered through the darkness in the direction of Snowdonia. The heaviness of the rain warned her that she must lose no time in getting over the ford. She had spent long enough in Wales to realise that the mountain streams could fill up very quickly and cause flooding on the lower land below. It was often more inconvenient than dangerous, but she might be trapped here if she didn't hurry.

The car started without any difficulty and she was sure the sound of the wind would cover any noise made by her departure. Slamming the car door, she reversed quickly away from the house, then turned sharply to make for the river. Just as she left, she threw a hasty glance over her shoulder and was panic-stricken to see Luke running from the house towards her. He was wearing what might have been pyjama trousers, but the light was so bad and she was in such a hurry, it was difficult to tell.

He was coming after her—she knew that for sure. As terror struck her, she heard him shouting something, his voice reaching her even above the whine of the wind. What he was shouting she couldn't make out, though no doubt he would be ordering her to come back.

Consequently, she put her foot down too hard on the accelerator and the car leapt forward at such a rate she was unable immediately to control it. The river, unfortunately, had risen well above its normal level, but she didn't realise that until she was in the middle of it. It was only then that she began to understand where her foolhardiness had led her. Her control of the small car was such that the steering wheel spun round in her hands, enabling the boiling, racing currents to push her easily from the narrow passage to the deeper waters beyond.

It wasn't a dangerous river, but, as in many similar places, the volume of water passing over the ford had, over the years, formed quite a deep pool. It was into this that Gay's car plunged, despite all her frantic efforts to prevent it.

I'm going to die, was the last thing she remembered thinking, as complete darkness closed over her. It was eerie. As the car came to rest on the bottom, she hit her head on something hard and screamed. Hysteria rose within her as she feared she would be entombed in the river for ever, without help. Using what must have been her last bit of sanity, she thrust open the car door, only to hear herself scream again as the murky waters swirled in and over her.

Afterwards she realised she probably owed her life to Luke. While she had managed to open the car door, the force of the water thrust her back when she tried to get out. It was Luke who caught her and dragged her forcibly from the flooded wreck, to bring her coughing and choking to safety on the shore.

Gay didn't immediately know what was happening, other than that she was in the arms of a powerful swimmer. Whoever was rescuing her had to be good, because the river was deep and full of debris, as well as running hard. When they reached the bank and he flung her on to it, she was barely conscious. Her chest hurt and all she could do was retch and groan.

Luke's hands were something less than gentle as he steadied her until she recovered slightly. Nor were they much kinder as they went over her, apparently searching for broken bones. Gay, perhaps mercifully half drowned, was only vaguely aware of his anger. Her chest hurt and her throat felt so raw she scarcely dared draw air into her deprived lungs. From somewhere above her came the rough sound of Luke's voice, the even rougher rasp of his breathing. The moan which escaped her frozen lips must have assured him she was still alive, but even so, he touched her wrist and heart with shaking fingers.

'Gay,' he said curtly, 'can you hear me? I'm going to carry you home, but you'll have to tell me if I hurt you.'

She nodded, still unable to speak. Cold and shock were making her teeth chatter and inducing a terrible numbness. Much as she tried to pull herself together, waves of darkness soon reduced her feeble efforts to nothing.

As Luke straightened and picked her up, she trembled violently. 'Don't try to talk,' he snapped tersely, as she struggled to find her voice. 'Give yourself time. You're shocked and hurt, but you'll recover.'

Will I? she wondered hazily, doubting it. He carried her carefully, so as not to jolt her too much over the rough ground, which couldn't have been easy as it was very dark and he had no torch.

'If only you'd stopped when I shouted,' he muttered brusquely, half to himself. 'You're so foolish in some ways, Gay.'

It was so true that she didn't try to deny it. Other things were worrying her more, but she wasn't yet in sufficient command of her senses to mention them, either. It wasn't far to the house, but she was so cold and miserable it felt like hours before they reached it.

Luke took her straight into the kitchen. 'It's warmer here, I should think, and less chance of damaging anything with our wet clothing.'

As she opened dazed eyes to stare at him, he lowered her almost gently to one of the wooden armchairs. 'Luke,' she croaked, aghast, 'what about the car?'

'What about it?' he asked briefly, passing her a measure of brandy from a bottle he found in a cupboard. 'I'd advise you to forget it, for the time being.'

'But you don't understand!' she babbled weakly, tears beginning to stream down her face. 'It's not mine, Luke. It belongs to my mother. However will I face her if we can't get it out? Oh,' she moaned distractedly, 'I'd have been better off drowned!'

'No, you wouldn't,' he said calmly, 'that wouldn't have solved anything. And if you're really bothered about the car, if it can't be got out I'll replace it for you. Now stop crying, for God's sake. There's enough water around as it is.'

'I—I can't help it . . .' she sobbed, feeling terribly sorry for herself. Luke was being kind but hard, and just then she felt desperately in need of comfort.

'Gay!' he exclaimed shortly, reaching for a large rough towel which lay near them, 'I'm quite aware of how you feel and I'm not unsympathetic, but right now it's more important to get you out of your wet clothes. You should have a hot bath—so should I, but the water was cold when I showered.'

'It's the cooker,' she attempted to explain. 'I allowed it to go out. At least, I forgot to build it up after supper.'

'My fault,' Luke shrugged, 'for hurrying you out of the kitchen so quickly. Does it light easily?'

'No,' she shook her head unhappily. 'It took me about all day yesterday to get it going.'

'It won't take me so long,' he promised grimly. 'We not only need baths, we need water for drinks and a hot water bottle. I presume you have one?'

Again she shook her drooping head. 'We believe in living Spartanly when we come here, and it's usually summer.'

His mouth suddenly tightened. 'Don't you allow for foolhardy people who run away in the middle of the night and plunge into rivers?'

Because this brought everything back, another wave of sickness came over her. 'Oh, please!' she choked, staggering to her feet, where all she could do was sway unsteadily as her legs refused to support her.

'Damn!' Luke muttered curtly, as though angry with himself for reminding her of something he had told her just moments ago to forget. Taking one glance at her grey face, he lifted her swiftly to the small cloakroom off the kitchen. 'Take it easy,' he murmured, setting her down, 'I expect you're still half full of river water.'

The sickness passed, but left her still so weak and trembling that Luke had to carry her back again.

'Now, let's tackle these wet clothes,' he said crisply.

'I can manage,' she assured him hastily, as he began removing her soaked jacket. As he paused, as though not convinced she could, her eyes fell waveringly on his bare chest. He was only wearing pyjama trousers, and colour flooded Gay's face as she realised how the wet silk of these clung revealingly to every line of his strong body. 'If you went upstairs,' she jabbered foolishly, 'and got rid of your own wet things, you could maybe bring me my dressing-gown.'

With a short sigh he turned abruptly and left her, but when he returned, not long afterwards, wearing his own dressing-gown and carrying hers, she was no further forward. Her fingers trembled so fiercely and felt so numb, she hadn't managed to undo even a single button. Unable to account for such a continuing weakness, she gazed at Luke helplessly with tear-drenched eyes.

He didn't need to be told, however. 'You'll have to let me,' he said curtly, watching her pale hands groping ineffectually.

'If you give me time . . .' she whispered protestingly, clutching her wet shirt defensively to her.

'Gay!' he exploded, his eyes glinting dangerously. 'Do you honestly want to get pneumonia? As it is, we've dithered around far too long. Haven't you sense enough to realise you're wet to the skin and there's no transport available if you get ill! No means at all of getting help, if you needed it, unless I was prepared to risk leaving you and walking six miles?'

'Help?' she repeated, her shocked brain unable to understand completely what he was saying.

'Something you're going to need very badly, if you won't be sensible.'

He looked so grim, she shuddered. 'I haven't been very sensible so far . . .'

'You can say that again!' he responded forcibly, taking hold of her and beginning to deal ruthlessly with her wet clothes.

'What do you think you're doing?' she wept.

'It must be obvious,' he retorted sharply, taking no notice of her copious tears as he peeled her thin sweater over her head. Next came her shirt and the rest followed until she stood before him, naked, shivering now with humiliation, as well as everything else.

'Luke . . .!' she appealed, her voice wobbling, her cheeks scarlet and hot, which felt peculiar when the rest of her was so cold. She would never forgive him for this, never, never, never! she told herself wildly, without knowing she was muttering half aloud.

Luke simply shrugged, unaffected by her helpless resentment, and got on with what he was doing. Taking hold of the towel, he rubbed the whole of her until she was glowing. Gay was too stunned to do anything but silently submit, but she couldn't help wondering if he had any idea what he was doing to her. For all she still felt ill, his hands on her body were bringing back feelings she had hoped never to experience again.

While he appeared unmoved, Luke's face was noticeably pale before he was completely satisfied she was dry and warmer. Wryly he put her into her robe and tied the sash. When she trembled, he asked severely, 'Did you think I was going to rape you?' When she made no reply, he snapped, 'I'd have to be pretty desperate for a woman before I'd attack a half drowned one. Besides, why should I, when we're going to be married?'

'Don't be silly,' she faltered, swaying in front of him, 'I wasn't thinking anything of the sort.'

For a moment, as he put out a hand to steady her, he watched her, his mouth compressed. 'I think,' he said slowly and enigmatically, a sudden gleam in his eye, 'you were more frightened of yourself. But,' he went on, before she could deny it, 'we won't go into that at the moment. I'm taking you to bed.'

As he carried her upstairs, Gay wondered dizzily how many more times she would be in his arms tonight. It must be becoming a habit, for over the past hour she never seemed to have been out of them. As he opened her bedroom door and laid her carefully on the bed, she opened confused blue eyes to look up at him.

He didn't meet her pleading gaze but concentrated on covering her quickly with blankets. She had a strange urge to apologise, to say meekly that she was sorry for all the trouble she had caused him, but the remoteness of his face, his obvious disinclination to look at her, made her change her mind.

'As soon as the kettle boils I'll bring you something hot,' he promised gravely.

The blankets were cold and she began shivering again, which she could see didn't please him. 'What about the fire in the lounge, Luke?' she asked. 'We forgot about that. Perhaps it's still alight.'

'No, it's not. I didn't forget about it,' he replied regretfully. 'It was out before I went to bed and I couldn't find any more logs.'

'I was going to saw some more up,' she frowned. 'There's enough wood in the shed across the yard.'

'Where it will have to remain until the morning,' Luke said firmly. 'I can't leave you, not in the state you're in, to start chopping wood tonight. I'll go and see what I can do in the kitchen first, anyway.'

He did get the fire in the cooker going and eventually brought her a cup of hot tea which she drank gratefully. It made her feel a little better, but the pervading cold in her body quickly destroyed any beneficial effect, and soon she was as cold as ever again.

Luke watched her with a worried frown. Her face was white and her teeth chattering. 'A holiday house which is only equipped as such is rarely a good place for an accident,' he sighed impatiently. As she continued to shiver convulsively, he added grimly, 'No electricity, not even a hot water bottle. You'll never be warm this side of Christmas!'

'It's my own fault,' she faltered wretchedly. 'I'm sorry, Luke. I wish now that I'd stopped when I heard you shouting.'

'You should have,' he agreed severely. 'Sometimes it even pays to think of others.' Leaning down, he touched her forehead. 'I'm just seeing if you have a temperature,' he said frostily, as her heavy eyes widened with fright. 'I don't think you have, but there's plenty of time.'

Because his irony hurt, somehow, she moved restlessly. 'I suppose next you'll be demanding to know why I ran away?'

'Don't you mean,' he observed dryly, 'that you're dying to tell me? I suppose it's because I behaved badly and you took fright, but I refuse to go into that tonight. For one thing, you're in no fit state, and I don't really feel much like it myself.'

'What if I try again?' Gay whispered defiantly.

'I don't think you'd get very far, not just now,' he drawled. 'Nor in the morning, by the looks of you.'

'I only wish I were warmer,' she whispered, unashamedly rubbing the tears from her eyes with the corner of the sheet. She tried to take no notice of his disapproving tones. He towered above her, so tall and decisive, while she didn't seem to have an ounce of fight left in her. 'It's all right for you,' she stammered fretfully, 'you can't imagine what it was like to plunge in the river, especially in someone else's car. I know I did wrong, but I'm paying for it. I think I might be going to die now of cold.'

'Oh, no you're not!' Suddenly, as though his mind was made up, Luke threw back the blankets and got in beside her. As she stared at him, so startled that she felt paralysed, he flung an arm around her then drew the bedclothes over both of them. 'This is the only way, Gay, and you must know it. If you don't get warm and keep warm you're going to be really ill.'

'But,' she shivered distractedly, 'what will people think?'

'That,' he exclaimed flintily, 'doesn't deserve an

answer.' He pulled her towards him as she immediately struggled to get out of bed. 'Come on, Gay,' he snapped, 'what's it to be? You can either freeze to death or sleep with me.'

'Which would be the lesser of two evils?' she spluttered, unable to remember when she had ever felt so alarmed.

'You must think of me as you like,' he retorted harshly, 'but I know which I would choose.'

'But you're not me!' she floundered, her mouth dry, as he went on holding her, the strength of his arm around her resembling an iron band.

'I'm willing to believe it,' he replied, so softly she could have hit him.

He held her so tightly she could scarcely breathe, and now her trembling wasn't entirely because of the cold. Luke would be flattered if he knew how swiftly heat was flooding her body. She had never been in bed with a man before, and, despite the rather unusual circumstances, she found the experience, on top of what she'd just been through, almost too much for her.

Silently he turned her round to face him. 'Come here,' he said, his voice terse. 'Won't you see sense, girl? This way we'll both soon be beautifully warm and, if it's important to you, no one need ever know.'

Jerkily she whispered, not altogether convinced. 'I—I still don't think it's a good idea.'

When again she strained away from him, he groaned. 'Do you think it's any easier for me?' In the dim glow of the oil lamp he smiled ironically, 'I'll try not to take advantage of the situation. You have my word that I intend waiting until we're married. Anyway, only a fool would try to take advantage of you in your present condition.'

She was bruised and shocked, but he could mean the way she looked? Gay bit her lip unhappily. Although dry, her hair was still tangled from Luke's rough towelling, and she feared her skin must still be tainted and smelling a little of river water. Despondently she whispered, 'I don't think many men would find me attractive in my present condition.'

'Oh, Gay,' he sighed, tightening his grip on her fractionally, 'don't be so silly! Why don't you forget about everything but getting warm? You know I'd find you attractive whatever condition you were in.'

How did one concentrate on getting warm? Gay wondered nervously. Odd spasms kept running through her and she shivered continually. Experimentally she moved her legs and cramp immediately seized them.

At her cry of distress Luke, swiftly comprehending, grasped the stricken limb and began massaging it with competent hands. The roughness of his palms soon brought a welcome relief as the knotted muscles relaxed. She wished she could as easily get rid of the feeling of his touch on her bare skin.

'That's fine now,' she said weakly, trying to push him away.

'You're sure?' he asked slowly, his eyes moving doubtfully to her face.

When she nodded restlessly, his eyes narrowed. Lying down again, he drew her to him, speaking against her averted cheek. 'You'd be wise to accept this, Gay. You're never going to feel any better unless you do, and I speak from experience. Once, when I was about your age, I was lost on a mountain. I'd been skiing and unfortunately taken an unfamiliar route. I was rescued and survived, but I still remember the cold, though most of the other details have faded. Like you, I imagined I would never survive. It was only as I got warm that I began believing I would.'

'I suppose I am being silly,' she said shakily.

'A bit,' he agreed, but mildly. 'Now how about trying to sleep?'

'I don't know why, but I don't feel like sleeping,' she muttered wearily. 'I feel exhausted but not sleepy. How can that be?'

'Reaction,' he said briefly, 'shock. You've just had a rather nasty accident.'

'But I'm not hurt,' she pushed impatiently away from him again. 'A little bruised, maybe . . .'

'Come here!' This time, as if refusing to put up with her endeavours to escape any longer, he put both arms around her, pulling her so close to his rugged frame she could scarcely breathe. When she began sobbing helplessly, he reached for a clean hankerchief and dried her cheeks, but went on speaking. 'What you've gone through tonight would have shattered most people. It's nothing to be ashamed of if you're feeling weepy. It's probably the best way of getting it out of your system.'

'I seem to have done nothing else since you pulled me out of the river.'

'Never mind.'

Finding Luke's voice and words infinitely soothing, she was content, for a moment, to lie in his arms without thinking. It was easier to blame cold and shock for the tremors that consumed her, rather than believe it had anything to do with Luke being here, in her bed. As she grew quieter, his hold gentled, but she was still aware of the strength of his hard body against hers. It began bothering her greatly that, as she became warmer, she found herself curving into him, as though her slender limbs sought the muscular contours of his, despite the restrictions she tried to put on them. It really shocked her when her arm reached out to find his waist and her hand touched his bare skin at the front of his dressing gown.

Rigidly she stiffened as he removed her hand and adjusted the cord on his robe. Resignedly, she heard him ask, 'What is it now?'

'Nothing,' she muttered feverishly. 'I wish you were

back in your own room, that's all. I don't like you being here.'

'As long as you don't dislike me,' he replied sardonically, 'I know it's nothing personal.'

'If I said I did, you wouldn't believe me,' she cried angrily.

'I might have to set about disproving it,' he warned, the sardonic note still in his voice as he asked, 'What happened to that arm that was creeping round my waist?'

'You pushed it away!' she exclaimed, thinking he had an incredible nerve even to mention it.

'I apologise.' She sensed he was smiling, which added to her feeling of outrage. 'You were snuggling up to me like a baby and for a moment I lost my nerve.'

'You told me I had to get warm,' she muttered, her cheeks hot. 'That was all I was trying to do. Do you think I'd try to get close to you otherwise?'

'Oh, I don't know.' Now his voice held a hint of mockery. 'I can recall one or two occasions when you even seemed to enjoy kissing me.'

Gay thought she would never be cold again as a wave of embarrassment engulfed her. How could Luke confront her with such an accusation when she wasn't really able to defend herself? 'I like kissing men, generally,' she retorted untruthfully.

As if to punish her, Luke's hand moved over her rib cage, coming to rest just under her breast. His eyes glinted at her sharply drawn breath and, as she turned to him with a gasp of protest, his mouth coolly descended to crush hers.

Frantically she tried to move away as his arms tightened involuntarily, then, to her surprise, she was free and he was at the other side of the bed.

'I'm sorry,' he said tightly, 'if my control's not what it should be, but you provoke me. I didn't intend kissing you, but at least it's got your circulation going. Your heart is beating like a drum.'

Angrily she turned her back on him, wondering why she hadn't thought of doing that before. What did he know about hearts when he didn't possess one? Hers might indeed be beating wildly, but it also ached so much it hurt. Luke appeared to accept her silence readily, almost as if he was relieved by it, and for a long time she lay considering this bitterly. Gradually, however, the warmth of his body behind her had a soothing effect. Eventually a drowsiness crept over her and she slept.

She woke to find the rain still beating against the window and Luke's breath on her face. She was in his arms again, her head pillowed on his shoulder, and when she turned to glance at him in some bewilderment, she saw he was also awake, watching her.

'Feeling better?' he asked, with a lazy smile.

Oddly enough, she returned his smile, curiously reluctant to leave his arms. He held her closely; she was warm and comfortable and wished wistfully she could stay like this forever. 'I think so,' she moved experimentally. 'My head's aching a little, but otherwise I seem to be all right.'

'You've probably caught a chill.' Gently he pushed the tumbled hair from her forehead and laid his hand on it. 'Hmm, you're warm but not hot. I think I'm going to keep you in bed, though. I can't afford to have you sick, with our wedding so near.'

Immediately she was jerked to her senses. Why did he have to spoil everything? 'Luke,' she faltered, 'I never agreed to marry you. Nor, I'm sure, do you really want to marry me, especially after last night. Remember,' she added despairingly, 'I'm the kind of girl who drives other people's cars into rivers!'

'One slightly crazy action,' he remarked mildly, with a grin, 'needn't necessarily mean you're permanently beyond hope. I believe we're compatible, which is the more important.'

'I don't think we are,' she denied.

He ignored her protest. 'That's one of the reasons why I'm determined to marry you.'

'We fight all the time, Luke.'

He shrugged. 'It adds spice to the cake.'

'Which might merely give us indigestion if we aren't friends,' she declared mutinously, feeling nervously that she was getting out of her depth. Luke's arms were still around her, which wasn't helping her to think clearly.

Tauntingly, he retorted, 'it depends what you consider matters most. I have one or two very good women friends whom I've never had the slightest desire to make love to. Yet I can't see why you and I can't be friends as well as lovers. We have a lot in common, which should help us. Marriage must be a challenge, as well as everything else. It has to be worked at. And even you, my small antagonist, must admit that something one takes time and trouble over is often more satisfying in the end.'

'I didn't ask to be read a lecture,' Gay muttered, adding bitterly, 'You only want to marry me because you feel it's time you took a wife. And you enjoy talking!'

His dark brows rose wryly. 'There are other things I'd rather be doing. Perhaps that's why I'm talking so much—to keep my mind off—er—other things?'

Flushing hotly, she jerked back, feeling the same temptation he hinted at moving inside her but unwilling to admit it. 'Are you going to stay here all day?' she asked.

'I'll get up and make breakfast,' he said curtly, aware of her sudden withdrawal. 'You lie still.'

'No,' she began protesting, then paused as he got swiftly out of bed. To have slept in his arms had been disturbing enough, but to see him standing beside her, clad only in a pair of pyjama trousers, made her realise fully just how close they had been. Inwardly she began trembling again and her throat went dry. Whatever happened she must get away; she didn't know how much more she could stand.

Nodding submissively, she slumped back against her pillows, but after he had gone she forced herself to her feet. Dismissing a peculiar weakness in her legs as temporary, she tried to take no notice of it. The shower, thanks to Luke's vigilance, was hot, and once dressed she felt better. She even managed to get halfway downstairs before she met Luke coming up them with two mugs of tea on a tray.

Mouth tightening, he came to a halt, rapidly assessing her over-pale face. 'Didn't I tell you to stay put for the time being?'

Luke wore dark slacks and a thin shirt with the sleeves rolled carelessly up to reveal brawny forearms. Even standing on a step below her he seemed to tower above her, making her feel insignificant. 'I've been in bed long enough,' she muttered. 'It was a kind thought,' she continued quickly, meeting the frank scepticism in his eyes, 'but I'm quite well enough to drink my tea in the kitchen.'

'Come on, then,' he appeared to give in without further argument although he still ran a professional eye over her. 'We'll soon see if the fuss was unnecessary.'

In the kitchen two things soon hit Gay like simultaneous blows. The first, that she was a lot more shaken than she'd thought: the second, that she couldn't leave without a car and, even if some other means of escape presented itself, she couldn't possibly go until her mother's car was safely out of the river.

'How long will it take to get it out, do you think?' she frowned, speaking almost to herself.

'Now what are you on about?' Luke sat down opposite her with a long-suffering sigh. 'A sore tooth?'

'Don't be so ridiculous!' she snapped at him irritably for being what she considered deliberately obtuse. 'I'm talking about Mummy's car—that's in the river. That's what I'm on about,' she cried belligerently, in an effort to hide her distress. 'When will you be able to do something about it? How long will it take you, do you think?'

'My dear girl,' he tilted his chair back on two legs, eyeing her infuriatingly, 'I'm not a horse, you know, nor do I happen to possess the type of heavy lifting equipment which I suspect will be needed for such a purpose.' He took a leisurely swallow of tea, gazing at her over the rim of the mug in a manner that set her teeth on edge. 'You'd need something in the nature of hydraulic lifting apparatus to move that car, if,' he stressed smoothly, 'it's at all possible.'

'H-hydraulic—what did you say?' she faltered.

'You heard,' succinctly.

'How—how much would that cost?' She stared at him, too stunned to try to hide her dismay.

'Well,' he pondered solemnly, 'you've got to get someone here first—a considerable distance. Then you have to persuade some poor chap to go down in possibly several feet of water to attach his lifting apparatus to the car. Then, if he's able to lift it, it will undoubtedly have suffered considerable damage. The whole exercise, with repairs, I should think, could be somewhere in the region of several hundred pounds.'

'Several—hundred pounds!'

Sardonically he nodded, viewing her wide, anxious eyes thoughtfully. 'I don't know about your insurance cover, of course. There's probably an exclusive clause in yours allowing for this kind of thing.'

Gay gazed at him with increasing horror, scarcely hearing his light sarcasm. 'I haven't got several hundred pounds. I haven't even got a hundred!'

'I didn't mention an exact sum,' he shrugged, adding with a bitter cynicism which startled her. 'Perhaps if you promised to go to bed with the chap, he might agree to do it for nothing?'

CHAPTER NINE

It was Gay's turn to be bitter. How could Luke speak to her like that? What on earth was going on in his mind? He might be desperate to have a wife from a family with a little prestige, but surely not even for this could he consider marrying a girl whom he didn't respect. Of course lots of men married girls who made no attempt to hide that they had had previous affairs, but she would never have thought Luke was the type who would. Perhaps, though, it was the wildly irresponsible life he imagined she had led, rather than her innocence, or lack of it, that bothered him?

The scarlet induced by his caustic remark faded, leaving her small face white. 'That was a beastly thing to say, Luke. Both an insult to me and whoever comes to help us.'

Luke was staring at her, his face grim. 'Yes it is,' he agreed surprisingly, with a sigh. 'Maybe I shouldn't have said it.'

'Just—maybe?' she cut in, her blue eyes suddenly blazing.

'Oh, forget it, Gay,' he said, impatiently frowning. 'I didn't mean to accuse you of being promiscuous. Somehow I don't think you are. If you have been overfriendly with men like David Douglas—and his wife did confirm it—I'll forget, given time.'

Hurt and frustrated, Gay whispered, 'I seem to have condemned myself from the start, and I suppose letting you stay in my bed last night hasn't helped.' He didn't reply and she rushed on recklessly, taking his silence for agreement. 'I told you to sleep elsewhere, didn't I? You forced yourself on me, and now you're saying it indicates that I'm used to sleeping with fellows!'

'You know why I insisted on sleeping with you last night,' he replied, expressionlessly, 'and I'd rather you didn't pretend you didn't like my being there. You clung to me most of the time as if you needed me, and I had a feeling that you'd done it all before.'

And it had been the first time she had slept with a man, let alone anything else! She knew she had curled up to him and clung to him, but that was because she loved him and had been cold. Anger at his misjudgment surged through her, and she let it, for it was the only thing which bolstered her pride.

'Perhaps you should compare notes with Nigel!' she said bitterly.

'No!' he exclaimed curtly, between his teeth, a hard colour coming over his cheekbones. 'Gay, shut up!'

'You brought it up,' she rejoined fiercely.

'Did I?' he muttered almost savagely, swinging away from her on a harsh breath. Going to the window, he looked out, and as he turned his head Gay thought his profile might have been carved out of stone. 'It's still raining,' he said over his shoulder, 'so I can't see any possibility of doing anything about your car today.'

Raising pain-darkened eyes, she met his dully as he came back to her. Why didn't pain become more endurable once one got used to it? 'So, how do we pass the time?' she asked, assuming a careless indifference. 'Sit in the lounge and argue, or play Scrabble?'

'Scrabble might be as safe as anything,' he said tersely, his grey eyes silver steel as he studied her. 'Do you feel up to cooking breakfast while I see to the lounge fire?'

'I'll do bacon and eggs and coffee,' she nodded, though doubting if she would be able to eat a thing.

'Two eggs and toast—and marmalade,' Luke grinned, on his way to the door. 'Oh, by the way,' he paused in the doorway, 'I brought a load of food last night, which I unpacked in the larder while I waited for the kettle to boil. I'd rather we pooled what we have, but if you don't feel so inclined, don't expect any of mine if yours runs out first.'

How could he swing so easily from anger to humour? His humour might have been a little forced, but it was more than she could manage! Nervously, Gay stared after him as he disappeared, feeling close to tears again. He hadn't even asked how she was. Well, not since they'd got up, which now seemed hours ago. Did this not prove he didn't care? If he had cared, even a little, she told herself, he would have been much more—she searched for the word—solicitous.

Wrinkling her forehead, Gay sighed heavily, feeling a breath of the previous evening's chill sweep over her. Then, making a great effort, she began cooking their breakfast. Hadn't she enough problems? Feeling sorry for herself wasn't going to solve any of them! Perhaps she should have remembered that a man with an empty stomach was seldom easy to deal with.

The morning passed with the deluge outside continuing, although the weather man, on Luke's battery radio, promised it would clear by late afternoon. They did play Scrabble in the lounge, but Gay, developing a feverish cold, fell asleep over the third game. She slept for several hours, wakening to find herself lying comfortably on the settee, covered by a large warm rug. Luke, she found, on gazing round in a dazed fashion, was stretched out in an armchair in front of a blazing fire, reading one of her father's paperbacks.

He must have been out chopping logs, she decided drowsily, for the basket was piled high and his hair was slightly damp, while his face had a hard, healthy glow.

Her eyes rested with some longing on the steaming cup of tea by his side. At that very moment he raised his eyes and caught her glance.

'Just in time,' he said. 'I've just made it, but I didn't want to wake you. Stay where you are and I'll pour you a cup.'

'This is the second time today that you've told me to

stay put.' Blushing, as she recalled the first time, she said hastily, 'What time is it? You shouldn't have let me sleep.'

'Why not?' he glanced at her keenly. 'I suspected you'd caught cold, after your ducking in the river, and rest is as good a cure as any.'

'I suppose so,' she agreed despondently, unable to find the energy to argue over it. What a mess she was in! Yet, as she drank her hot tea, her spirits did revive a little. 'If only it would stop raining!' she sighed, hearing it still falling outside.

'It must do, eventually,' Luke replied idly, as though he didn't really care whether it did nor not.

'What can we do until it does? I mean, seriously. We can't play Scrabble all day.'

'You aren't doing a thing!' He was suddenly grim. 'I've been worried enough.'

Gay blinked at his harsh tone but decided not to believe him. 'At least let me get dinner,' she begged.

Eventually he gave in. 'I'm afraid I ate the remains of the chicken for lunch, but I did bring some steak. How about that?'

'You'll get fat,' Gay warned fretfully, hating to be reminded of the previous evening and refusing to be drawn into a better mood.

'Once the weather clears I'll soon walk it off,' he grinned, not taking her remark seriously.

'Luke,' she asked unhappily, over dinner, 'when you were out did you see if you could find the car?'

He grimaced wryly. 'Yes,' he admitted, 'apart from anything else I was curious. I went after you'd fallen asleep this morning, while I was out chopping logs.'

'And . . .?'

'I'm afraid it must still be there, but the river's running so high it was impossible to see it.'

Gay drew a deep breath, keeping herself under control. If she tried hard she might be able to manage something sensible. 'Apart from anything else, it might have been useful to have had a car here.'

'By anything else, you mean running away?'

Silently she nodded, surprised that Luke had mentioned it. His face was grim and he had avoided talking about the car, as though it were the plague. Yet somehow, although she had broached the subject herself, she had no wish to continue discussing it. Preparing dinner had taken a lot out of her, which she found disconcerting as normally she had an abundance of vitality.

'Would you mind if I went to bed?' she asked, as he made no further comment and they finished their coffee.

He didn't argue, but his eyes narrowed. 'You're sure you're feeling better?'

'Quite sure.' She raised her silken head to smile at him coolly. 'I'm just tired.'

'Go on, then,' his mouth twisted in a smile that just about matched her own, 'I'll bring you some hot milk when you're ready for it, but I'm sure that's all you'll need from me tonight.'

Gay was relieved that Luke didn't suggest sleeping with her again, yet she was aware of a strange disappointment. That, she told herself, was both ridiculous and stupid. All day he had kept his distance with a vengeance. He had scarcely touched her, and then only her forehead with impersonal fingers, to see if she were hot. He was obviously determined to keep his distance, and she was ashamed that she didn't feel as grateful as she thought she should have been.

Sighing, in some confusion, she went wearily to bed, and though Luke did arrive with the promised hot milk, he stayed no longer than two or three minutes.

The next day, to her dismay, she was forced to stay in bed as her cold was worse instead of better. So it was longer than she expected before she was able to get out and search for the car. During the time she was ill Luke nursed her competently but remotely, only his eyes had occasionally betrayed his concern. His determination to avoid touching her continued, and if to begin with she found this reassuring, it eventually aroused in her a resentment which she found difficult to understand.

It was this confusion of spirit that drove her out of bed the following morning. 'I've been there long enough,' she told an angry Luke, who caught her again on her way downstairs. 'I really am better this time and I must go and see if I can find the car.'

Although he quite clearly disapproved, he didn't actually try to stop her, but he did insist that she had some breakfast before she even thought of doing anything.

'You've been quite ill,' he said shortly, 'I should really bundle you back upstairs, but I'll be a coward and give in. I'll let you stay, I'll even come with you and help look for the car, if you promise to try to eat something first.'

'I'd like to thank you for looking after me so well,' Gay said stiffly, as she crunched her way through a thin slice of toast. She felt well but weak. The weakness bewildered her greatly, for it was worse when Luke looked at her.

He shrugged, staring at her tight-lipped. 'It was the least I could do, especially as indirectly I have to be responsible for your cold.'

'So remorse makes a good nursemaid?' She tried to be flippant, only, from the expression on Luke's face, he wasn't in the right mood for careless jokes.

As they left the house an hour later, he revealed a piece of information which surprised her. 'I might have found your car yesterday, but I couldn't leave you to look farther down the river.'

Gay stumbled, glancing at him quickly. Why couldn't he have left her? She had been feverish, inclined sometimes, to delirium, but he hadn't seemed terribly concerned. Not until now did it occur to her that while Luke might not have been particularly loving he had, in fact, rarely left her side.

Then, as she pondered over his words, apprehension

replaced curiosity. Why did he talk as though the car was gone from the ford? 'Luke,' she whispered, her face paling with shock, 'you don't think it could have been swept away, do you?'

Unfortunately it had been. Almost half a mile from the ford, they found it lying on a bed of rocks, at the foot of a waterfall. Gay swayed, clutching Luke's arm for support, as she stared down at the wreck—for that was the only way in which the small car could now be described—for a full minute before turning desperately away. It had belonged to her mother and would never be fit to drive again. That much was clear, if nothing else.

'Gay?'

She raised eyes dazed with tears and defeat, unable to speak but feeling grateful for his terse tones. If he had been tenderly sympathetic she knew she would have broken down completely.

'If you stay here,' he said calmly, 'I'll go and take a closer look.'

He left her quickly, as much, she sensed, to give her time to pull herself together as to examine the broken vehicle below. Even through tear-filled eyes she could see it was only fit for scrap.

When Luke returned she had achieved some degree of composure but her mouth began trembling again when he merely shook his head. 'We'd better inform the police as they might easily imagine someone has had an accident and been injured or killed. Apart from that I'm afraid there's not much we can do. It's so firmly wedged between those two boulders, it would take a fortune to salvage and wouldn't be worth it. It's squashed like a sardine tin.'

'Don't spare me!' Gay cried bitterly, putting her hands over her ears.

'I'm sorry, Gay. I would if I could, but you must be able to see with your own eyes, and would it make you feel any better if I pretended the damage wasn't as great as it looks?'

Bleakly she shook her head. 'No, forgive me . . .'

He took her arm, his grip oddly comforting. 'A few more floods like the one we've had and there won't be much of it left. By the end of summer probably no one will be able to tell what it was, but if it's going to worry you, Gay, I can easily find men and equipment to remove it.'

'No one ever comes here,' Gay replied dully. 'It's fairly inaccessible, and the beauty spots are all farther down towards Cwn Col.'

Luke nodded, then turned her away, taking her back to the house. Once inside, he closed the door and, after putting her in a chair by the fire, poured her a drink. 'It's no use fretting.' He placed the glass in her hand, his eyes on her tear-stained face.

'Can't you find anything else to say but that?' she muttered fiercely, her numbing lassitude dispersing in sudden anger at his apparent inability to understand the predicament she was in. 'If it had been my car I would have agreed with you, but it isn't. How on earth am I supposed to explain this to my mother? Do I say,' she blazed at him bitterly, 'darling Luke and I quarrelled and I ran out on him—straight into the river?'

'Why not?' He watched her distraught face cautiously. 'Although I would stick closer to the truth if I were you, then I can more easily take the whole blame and buy your mother a new car. You can say you were worried about your reputation and decided to leave in the middle of the night as otherwise your devoted fiancé might have tried to prevent you. As only your parents happen to know where you are, it ought to be easy.'

Gay sniffed away another tear. What Luke said might make sense, but he sounded cynical. 'Mummy won't accept a new car.'

'I'm sure she will, from me.'

Unhappily, Gay fixed her eyes on his hard, confident face. That he was used to dealing expertly with emergencies was obvious. Clearly he didn't intend losing any sleep over this one. Once a new car was safely delivered he would no doubt forget all about it.

'You'll only use this to strengthen your hold over me,' she whispered, wondering how he always managed to get the better of her.

'We'll see,' he replied tautly. 'I still want you for my wife, Gay.'

'Just because I am who I am,' she choked, jumping mutinously to her feet. 'You're so sure of yourself, of what you want, you'd be willing to marry a girl who dislikes you?'

'What did you say?' he snapped, his eyes glinting dangerously. 'Don't throw too many wild statements around or I might just set out to show you how wrong you are.'

Absurdly tense, she stared at him, her eyes widening. Dizzily she fluctuated between misery and anger. Despair won, bringing one hand to her heart to hide its dull thudding, while the other went involuntarily to the man by her side. 'Luke!' she cried tearfully, almost falling into his arms.

To begin with, all he did was hold her closely until her sobs quietened. He appeared not to mind having her cry on his shoulder. He even smoothed her hair, pressing light kisses on her forehead and cheeks. It was only as she became calmer that his kisses changed. Then his hand cupped her chin, lifting her face a little so he could avail himself of her trembling mouth. At first he was quite gentle, but not for long. Soon her quivering response had his arms tightening, his mouth exploring with growing insistence, his hands moving from breast and waist to the slender curves of thighs.

He didn't speak, and for this Gay felt oddly grateful, for she feared he might ask cynically if her clinging arms was her way of expressing dislike. As he didn't love her she didn't want tender words from him either. Her tears had stopped, but her control was still precarious. If he was too gentle she might lose it altogether.

Luke muttered something thickly and went on kissing her. She tried to push him away, but her mind, as on other occasions, refused to co-operate with her body. He must be as aware as she was of the deep flow of passion between them, because she could feel the rapid thud of his heart, his increasingly difficult breathing. He must be as conscious of the dangerous rise of desire, welding them together, rapidly becoming unmanageable.

Gay must have been right in her hazy deductions, as Luke stiffened abruptly, his mouth lifting from the responsive warmth of her own. But, as though unable to let her go, he groaned and buried his face in the curve between her shoulder and throat and she felt the heat of his mouth against her skin. Then his hands were pushing up under the thin wool of her v-necked sweater, their probing, unhurried movements as erotic as his mouth, throwing her into a whirlpool of sensuous desire. The next moment her arms were around his neck, her fingers lacing their way through his thick dark hair, and she was clutching him to her fiercely.

'God!' she heard him exclaim, his voice muffled despairingly. Yet he continued still to hold her, until the searing pressure of his arms and lips began hurting. It was a pain mixed with hunger, but not a hunger that mere kisses could assuage, and they both knew it.

Luke's face had a grey tinge as he suddenly raised his head. The tightness of his arms relaxed, although he retained a light hold, as if it was important to see her face. 'What am I to you, Gay?' he asked tersely.

Lifting heavy lashes, she gazed at him in a daze. She heard him, but was too overwhelmed by her emotions to immediately understand what he was saying. Luke stared at her, the darkness of his usually silvery eyes confusing, which didn't help her to think clearly, Bleakly, when she did manage to pull herself together, she realised she couldn't answer him with the complete honesty he appeared to demand. That would be too much. She hadn't the courage to face his possible laughter. 'I don't have to answer that,' she replied evasively, looking away from him.

'I won't wait for ever,' he retorted savagely. 'You must know that, whatever your own feelings. I can't be tormented much longer.'

'Aren't you the one who's doing the tormenting?' she whispered, scarcely aware of what she might be betraying. She wanted to leave him but couldn't bring herself to make the decisive move.

His hands were restless on her shoulders, gripping the bone painfully, as though not entirely conscious of what he was doing. His tall body was tense. 'This—what we have now, isn't enough, and you know it.'

She was ashamed that she did. Colour stealing to her cheeks, she whispered, 'I'm not a child, Luke!'

'What's that supposed to mean?' he snapped harshly. 'I know you're not and so do you, but that's never stopped you making a convenience of your age.'

She glanced at him again, her eyes bewildered. 'Riddles,' she muttered. 'You're talking in riddles!'

'No!' he attacked with a curtness which frightened her. 'You understand all right. When it suits you, you pretend you're too young to make decisions.'

'Like . . .?'

His furious glance scorned her weak evasiveness. 'Like whether or not to ask me to make love to you properly before we're married. You're leaving the initiative to me, and whichever way I choose would be wrong. If I followed my inclinations you could make my life hell afterwards, or probably leave me, which would be the same thing.'

Gay found it difficult to follow his reasoning. It was only obvious that he continued to misjudge her true character. Perhaps this wasn't entirely his fault, but she had no wish to go into that just now.

Biting her lip, she asked uncertainly, 'How could I

affect your life, one way or another?'

'You know the answer to that as well,' he grunted, adding, with a kind of savage violence while his eyes scorched her, 'Heaven help me, but I have only to look at you! I don't know what kind of power you exert, but I hope you don't think I enjoy it?'

'Power?' she queried, wondering if this was really Luke talking. 'Like what?'

'Like this!' he exclaimed, his voice roughening. Fiercely he jerked her close again, his mouth taking hers. He took her by surprise, catching her off balance, and the pressure of his mouth forced her lips apart in an assault of undisguised passion.

With a sharp wrench she stepped away from him, slapping his hard cheek with an angry hand. The way he kissed her had been an insult. 'Why not try thinking of me as the plain little nobody you first took me for? That might help restore your peace of mind!'

'Gay!' he cut in broodingly, lifting a hand briefly to his face and then dropping it again.

'Remember Miss Dalmonte?' Gay rushed on heedlessly, her rage driven by pain. 'You fancied her, but she wouldn't have you, and you lost yourself a prize. Compared with her, I'm very small fry indeed. But if you waited, I'm sure, with what you've got, you'd soon have plenty of society girls queueing up for your hand.'

Gay had never seen him looking so forbidding, not for a long time. For a moment she feared he was going to strike her, as she had just hit him, but instead he contented himself with a remark so full of contempt it made her shrivel. 'Sometimes,' he snapped, 'I find it almost impossible to believe you haven't stepped out of the nearest gutter! The way you express yourself on occasion will have to change. Will most certainly change,' he assured her coldly, 'once you're married to me.'

Her eyes stayed on his taut face. If she had hoped to hide her love for him it appeared she had succeeded beyond her wildest expectations. He really believed she was a natural little hoyden and despised her as such, for all he was still apparently determined to marry her.

Gathering her resources into a cold stare, she muttered rebelliously, 'I wouldn't rely on it. Can a leopard change his spots?'

Luke stepped back, his face stony as he drew a sharp breath. 'We're getting out of here, Gay, just as soon as you can pack.'

'What? Now?'

'Yes, back to London.' His voice was strained but there was no mistaking the thread of steel. 'It's what you want, isn't it?'

'Of course.' Hadn't she risked her life trying to get away, the other night? Why then, when she was offered another chance, did she feel reluctant to take it? Nothing had altered. If anything Luke and she were even farther apart.

He said flatly, ignoring her slight hesitation and brief but uncertain glance, 'You made a mistake in coming here on your own, but I made a greater one in coming after you. However, there's nothing to stop us going home, where I can endeavour to put things right as soon as possible. To begin with I'll buy your mother a new car. Whether you want to marry me or not is immaterial at the moment, but for your parents' sake we'd better decide to become at least temporarily engaged. Who knows,' he concluded, with a bitter quirk, 'you might eventually consider taking me on permanently.'

'No, thank you,' she said stiffly, feeling very cold. 'I refuse to become a prop for your reputation, or your image.'

'Do you really think I need one?' he snapped repressively.

'No,' she replied shortly, 'but it's something to do with ambition, isn't it, rather than necessity.'

He said tersely, 'Once I had you I might be content.'

'You might be?' She was pierced by pain and an

insane desire to laugh. 'That's a gamble I'm not prepared to take. Miss Dalmonte wouldn't have you and you're making do with me, but once you recovered from the shock of her rejection you might become even more ambitious. A man like you mightn't know where to stop!'

'Neither do you!' he rejoined, his eyes dark with an anger that made her retreat a nervous step. He looked curiously driven and she cared nothing for his cruel, ironic smile. Suddenly she dared not say another word as something warned her that if she did he might not be responsible for his actions.

'Gay,' he said grimly, with an irritable, impatient gesture, 'go and get ready, before you say anything more. I've grown tired of listening to you.'

She went, unwillingly, unhappily aware of his icy withdrawal. She sensed his contempt and was secretly tortured by it, while aware that somehow she must find the strength to go along with his plans, if only for a few days.

Quickly they packed everything up, damped down the cooker and left everything tidy. By the time they were ready to leave the fire in the cooker was completely out and, though relieved, Gay spared it a last wistful glance. She had intended cooking something nice for Luke's supper, but now they wouldn't be here.

They walked to the main road where Luke managed to secure a lift by waving down a lorry. Soon they were dropped near the garage in the town where Luke had left his car and were on their way to London.

Sitting beside Luke, in luxurious comfort, Gay began feeling sick. She was sure she wasn't going to be actually ill again, but she did feel tired and weary.

'Another mistake,' Luke's glance flickered sideways over her white face. 'You weren't fit to come out, let alone face a journey to London.'

'You insisted,' she said dully.

'I suppose we could have stayed.'

'We needn't have rushed away like this!'

His ears caught her unconscious resentment and his glance lingered curiously before he gave his attention to the road. 'Perhaps you should have explained how you felt. Never mind, I'll find a hotel. We don't have to reach London tonight.'

'I'd rather,' she said quickly, fearing she had betrayed too much.

'Please be guided by me,' he replied coldly. 'Your mother's car is a wreck. I'd better return you in a more reasonable condition.'

Despite his rather terse attempts to lighten the atmosphere, Gay was quick to note a change in him that almost amounted to hostility. 'You needn't worry about that,' she shrugged. 'Mummy warned me that if I insisted on leaving home I'd have to learn to stand on my own feet. I expect that covers dealing with men as well as everything else.'

'Which you do admirably, up to a point,' he allowed cynically, 'then you panic and run away.'

Gay frowned. He must be alluding to her behaviour at the cottage. Heat came to her cheeks as she remembered how, when Luke had kissed her, she had clung to him. To her shame, she could have sworn it wasn't she who had done the running. On at least two occasions it was Luke who had withdrawn first.

Following a vague line of thought, she said slowly, 'You hinted that it wasn't easy for you to be at the cottage. I imagined you meant because of your work?'

'Not that,' he replied curtly.

'Then what were you complaining about?' she asked confused.

'I wasn't complaining,' he snapped, increasing his speed impatiently to pass a loitering motorist. 'I found the whole situation more difficult to handle than I expected, but I wasn't aware I'd complained.'

'Are you tactfully suggesting it was I who was difficult to manage?' she frowned.

'No, it wasn't you,' he replied grimly. 'at least not

directly. Now be a good girl,' he spoke more evenly, 'and let me concentrate on my driving, so I can reach the hotel I'm thinking of before you collapse.'

It was over a hundred and forty miles to London, but long before they had covered half that distance Gay was tired. After stopping for lunch they went on a little farther until just outside Swindon Luke decided they would stop for the night.

He chose a hotel in a quiet spot, surrounded by large grounds and half hidden by tall trees. He must have been here before, Gay thought, otherwise he could never have found it. As he booked in she stood to one side, studying him. He looked tired and rather strained. It was partly because of this that she hadn't insisted on going on. Suddenly she knew a strange urge to consider Luke before herself. It wasn't that she was unfeeling, it was just that usually he was so proficient he never appeared in need of anyone's sympathy.

Now she felt a continuing remorse. He hadn't had much of a break—if that was why he had come to Wales. Whatever the reason, he hadn't enjoyed himself. That much was obvious.

She noticed the glances of the hotel staff. All evening she was conscious of women regarding him with hidden admiration. Some, in fact, stared at him openly, while they regarded Gay with envy. Not for the first time did Gay wish he wasn't so attractive. His dark good looks and self-assurance appeared to get him attention wherever he went.

'I'll see you to your room, Gay,' he said coolly.

When she glanced up she found his eyes fixed on her, and something in their depth made her tremble. For once she didn't argue. Terribly aware of him, she rose to her feet obediently. Putting a proprietorial hand under her arm, he guided her from the lounge, where they had sat since having dinner. Luke had drunk steadily, but she hadn't been able to find the courage to rebuke him, although she had stuck pointedly to orange juice herself. It was the unhappy conviction she had had that his drinking had something to do with her which kept her silent.

They had talked spasmodically, and only about Wales. Gay was surprised to learn, though he had already mentioned he had been there before, that he knew it well. He was, she discovered, much more familiar with it than she was. He could name many of its most famous beauty spots without even pausing to think. It didn't surprise her, though, when he confessed that his visits, over the last few years, had been mostly to the industrial areas. And then he always flew, rather than travelling by car.

'Business seems to take you all over the world, just about everywhere,' she said flatly. Tomorrow he would be back with his secretary, the super-efficient Miss Carson. Already Gay could see his office doors closing against her and felt an irrational fear. 'Your wife might very rarely see you,' she muttered, 'that's if you had one.'

'She could come with me,' he replied narrowly, his eyes on her glowing red hair. 'I don't intend travelling so much when we're married, though.'

Gay thought of this as they went upstairs together. She could feel the pressure of his hand on her arm sending fiery messages to every part of her, and it was all she could do to prevent herself from turning to him and throwing herself into his arms.

He opened her bedroom door for her and she had to be thinking of his last remark just then. Minutes later, it could still bring colour to the exhausted paleness of her face.

His gaze seemed to concentrate curiously on her flushed cheeks, seeking the reason for her increased colour. He entered her room but didn't close the door. 'Can you manage to get undressed?' he asked, frowning.

'Of course!' she stammered, her cheeks pinker than ever.

'I was going to ask a maid to help you,' he said tersely. 'I know you wouldn't want me. Or do you?'

She guessed he had had rather too much to drink, although he had every appearance of being stone cold sober. Luke wasn't like normal men, she thought bitterly, he would always be in complete control of his faculties. It was the cynical note in his voice as he asked his last question that made her wonder.

'I can manage,' she repeated woodenly.

'Have a good night's rest, then,' he watched her expressionlessly, 'you still look all in. I shouldn't have dragged you away.'

'Why did you—truly, Luke?' she asked impulsively.

'Maybe because I'm not so invincible as I thought,' he replied enigmatically, going quietly out and closing the door.

CHAPTER TEN

AFTER a leisurely breakfast they left the hotel to complete their journey to London. Luke insisted that they lunched on the way and took their time over this as well. His consideration might have been comforting if Gay hadn't felt the impatience beneath it. For some reason which she couldn't fathom, Luke was tense.

She felt a little this way herself. London presented problems and somehow the end of an era. In London Luke would change. Not much, she told herself ironically. Here he was a caring stranger—in town he would become a grim-eyed, businesslike one. If they had to be engaged it wouldn't be for long. Afterwards he would disappear from her life. It might not happen overnight, but she couldn't stay engaged to him indefinitely. Eventually they must split up.

Gay frowned as she watched the first approaches to London appearing. Wasn't that what she wanted? She couldn't understand her own doubts. Luke intended marrying her only because she was suitable. He didn't love her. Why then should the prospect of not seeing him again make her feel miserable?

He didn't take her straight home. He went to his apartment first, and she asked him why.

'I want to use the phone and it will be easier from here,' he replied. 'There's also the matter of your engagement ring. You must have one.'

'You—you want us to go shopping for it?' Gay paused in dismay, having reluctantly allowed herself to be persuaded to leave the car.

'No,' he said coldly, hustling her inside, 'I already have it.'

'Weren't you taking a lot for granted?' she exclaimed, glancing at him resentfully.

'We've discussed all this,' he snapped, 'so don't begin pretending you had no idea. Shopping for the ring is fine for people in love, but if they're not it can be quite embarrassing.'

'You sound as if you'd done it before,' she queried curiously, suddenly taut.

'I haven't,' he snapped, 'but I can use my imagination.'

The sarcasm in his voice didn't escape her. As he turned away, she gazed nervously at his stiff back. 'Why didn't you bring the ring to the cottage?'

His broad shoulders lifted imperceptibly. 'I realised you needed time to get used to the idea, so I decided to postpone the formalities until we returned here.'

'You mean the chain round my neck, don't you?' she muttered sulkily, in an effort to restrain a more forceful feeling of alarm.

'I was only thinking of a ring round your finger,' Luke retorted coolly, 'just as a way of letting the world know you belong to me.'

Gay flinched at that, her face going pale. 'You have to put a stamp on everything you own?'

'Sometimes it pays,' he replied, almost insolently, his eyes flickering over her as they went to his study. 'There are other ways besides a ring, but those we can pursue later.'

For a moment something in his eyes frightened her and she was thankful to sink down in the nearest chair while he rang for tea. While waiting for his rather startled domestic staff to fetch it, he rang a garage and ordered a new car to be delivered to Gay's mother next day.

'Just like that?' Gay gasped, when he finished.

'No problem,' he said briefly. 'Now you can forget about it.'

'We still have to explain about it!' she protested.

'You can leave that to me as well,' he answered curtly, 'I'm responsible.'

It was easier to believe he was, and he seemed able to stand any amount of responsibility. He was, she supposed, used to it. His eyes glinted and she felt a tingling sensation as they went over her, and her fingers tightened. If she loved him would she feel this way? Surely love was a calm, placid emotion, not this fierce desire which alternatively made her wildly angry or full of despair—a feeling which had her either wanting to fight him or throw herself into his arms.

About the car she continued to feel guilty. Luke had come to Wales in search of his fiancée. He might have been genuinely worried that she was staying at a remote house on her own. He also believed she was the kind of girl who wouldn't mind spending a few nights alone with a man. Gay sighed. After David and Jim and the way she had appeared to live she could only blame herself that he had gathered such impressions. No—it wasn't Luke's fault that she had panicked and run. She realised now that she would have been safer with him than in the river. As it turned out, he had saved her life, but surely he couldn't expect her to give him the rest of it in order to pay for it?

'Don't start and brood about the weekend,' he snapped, passing her a cup of tea, 'otherwise you'll never be able to forget it.'

'Perhaps I don't want to forget it,' she said tensely.

Without replying Luke went abruptly to his desk where he unlocked a drawer and took out a ring. Gay noticed his own tea was untouched.

'Here, try this for size.' He came back to her and picked up her hand, slipping the ring on her finger.

Startled, she stared at the dazzling piece of jewellery, the brilliance of the stone. For a moment she forgot the antagonism between them. 'Why, it's beautiful, Luke,' she faltered huskily. 'It must have cost a fortune!'

'I can afford it,' he drawled with a dry grimness. 'I can supply the dazzle, if you like, the mink and the Rolls. The rest is up to you.'

At the derision in his voice her pleasure in the ring faded. Why did he have to spoil everything with his habitual cynicism? Swiftly she lowered eyes wide with hurt. She hadn't meant to refer to the price of the ring, but she had been at loss to find another way to cover an overwhelming surge of emotion. For a moment she had forgotten why he wanted to marry her. When she had remembered it knocked all such romantic notions from her head.

If, in haste, she had blundered, Luke gave her no opportunity to put things right. With a quick change of mood he began making phone calls, apparently about business, leaving her to drink her tea alone.

A short while later he took her home. They talked to Patricia Fenton in the lounge in the comfortable house where the Fentons had lived since coming to London some years ago. To begin with, Patricia was startled and anxious over what had happened at the cottage, but Luke soon reassured her. He was an expert in diplomacy, Gay realised, lowering her eyes to hide her bitterness. Few women might be immune to his dark charm, not even her mother. Patricia, she could see, was well on the way to becoming devoted to him. Gay doubted, if she had tried to explain her adventures in Wales, that Patricia would have been half as tolerant as she was with Luke.

Patricia, when it came to it, accepted Luke's gift of a new car with a kind of charming, grateful helplessness of which Luke obviously wholly approved. Lady Fenton asked him back for dinner, when he rose to take his leave, and when he agreed she was delighted.

'Luke and I are going to get on well,' she said happily, when she and Gay were alone. 'We're all very lucky, aren't we, darling? You're getting a wonderful husband and your father and I a wonderful son-in-law.'

Abruptly Gay cut short Patricia's unusual effusiveness. 'Why did you tell him where I was?' she demanded.

'Oh, that?' Patricia did look briefly uncomfortable. 'Well, I—I didn't feel I could do anything else. You must admit, Gay, that when your fiancé wants to know something he's almost impossible to put off. If I hadn't told him where you were I think he would have persisted until I did.'

'You could have tried not telling him,' Gay suggested confusedly.

Patricia frowned. 'He's a very determined man, dear. Actually I did pretend at first that I didn't know where you'd gone to, but he acted so strangely I'm afraid I grew nervous.'

Incredulously, Gay exclaimed, 'You mean he threatened you?'

'No, dear, of course not. It was—oh, just something in his face. And when he said you were engaged—well, what could I do? It was naughty of you not to tell me before you went away. It made me feel an awful fool—and very hurt!'

Gay listened in silence for several minutes, feeling unable to defend herself while her mother gently scolded her. 'As for the river,' Patricia rounded off, 'it was silly of you to forget how quickly it floods. Your father will throw a fit! It's a good job you managed to get out of the car in time.'

'Yes,' Gay nodded, relieved now that neither she nor Luke had corrected Patricia's assumption that there had been no one in the car when it was swept away. Gay's father might not have been so easily put off, but at the moment he was far too busy to look too closely into his daughter's affairs.

That evening Gay took extra care over dressing. It was only, she decided, because her parents liked her to look nice, it had nothing at all to do with Luke! His ring felt heavy on her finger, making her achingly aware of it. The sooner she was rid of it the better, she told herself, while her hands clenched involuntarily against such a thought.

Luke arrived at seven-thirty. Gay retreated hastily, with a fast beating heart after, she supposed, he dutifully kissed her. His mouth and hands lingered until she drew back. It didn't take a very discerning eye to see that both her parents were extremely pleased about her engagement. Luke fitted in so well, appearing to establish an immediate rapport. How, she wondered bleakly, as her heart steadied to normal, would they take it when she and Luke parted?

It should have been a very congenial occasion. They drank champagne and Patricia said they should really have had a party and she wished Morris and his new wife could have been here.

'You've met my stepson, I presume?' she asked Luke at dinner. 'He looked after Gay while we were in Paris, until Gay joined us to look after me. We didn't want to leave her in London,' she went on, not seeming to notice Gay's attempt to change the subject, 'but she was trying to make a few decisions about her future, then she had this part-time job in a boutique.'

Luke frowned but made no comment, and Gay knew her mother merely assumed he didn't care for the idea of her working.

'Oh, by the way, dear,' as though at last realising another topic might do better, Patricia turned to her daughter, 'I forgot to tell you I had a letter from Katrina. She and David are settling down nicely—she's quite thrilled with everything. Both she and David send their love. David Douglas is Gay's cousin,' she explained to Luke, entirely unaware of dropping a miniature bomb. 'He married the daughter of one of our closest friends and Gay often babysits for them.'

'Wasn't she there just before they went abroad?' Luke asked, with apparent interest, while Gay felt like sinking through the floor.

'I believe she was,' Patricia exclaimed. 'You were, weren't you?' she glanced at Gay with a smile. 'You helped her out with a rather important dinner party—you pretended to be the maid or something, Katrina said, and then looked after the children while they went to a wedding.'

'Why didn't you tell me?' Luke asked furiously, when later her parents left them to themselves.

'Because it might have spoiled everything for David. We didn't know,' Gay replied coldly.

'It was a ridiculous thing to do!' he exclaimed.

'I agree,' she retorted, every nerve in her body strung tight, now that the moment of discovery had arrived. 'But you were really responsible for the situation. You were looking Katrina over and she had to make a good impression.'

Luke said tersely, 'What on earth made her think I go in for that sort of thing? Does she imagine I spend my time vetting the wives of employees? It was entirely for my aunt's sake that I agreed to dine with your friends that evening.'

'But David said . . .' Gay began.

'I don't care what Douglas said—or his wife thought,' Luke interrupted curtly. 'They maybe did believe they were doing the right thing, asking me to dinner and doing everything in style, including a maid. You had me fooled, at that,' he admitted harshly. 'Even when I learnt who you were I still believed you'd been working as a kind of glorified au pair girl.'

'You even left me a tip,' Gay glared at him. 'Ten whole pounds! You were so damned patronising I could have sunk through the floor. I still have it.'

'I was trying to find out if you were the girl I'd met that morning. You looked different, but when your eyes met mine there was the same feeling. Do you think I usually go round tipping the domestic staff each time I go out to dinner?'

'I think you were trying to put me in my place and

keep me there!' Gay exclaimed angrily.

'You could be right,' he surprised her by confessing grimly.

Gay frowned, briefly confused, then attacked again. 'Instead of promoting David, you sent him abroad. Why?'

'I thought he was too interested in you,' Luke snapped. 'A wink between cousins is one thing, between employer and maid quite another.'

Ignoring the bleakness in his grey eyes, Gay drove herself to ask mockingly, 'I wonder how you could spare the time to even glance in my direction. You were so busy pursuing Miss Dalmonte.'

He sighed impatiently. 'I wanted to know you . . .'

'For amusement,' Gay cut in sharply. 'Lily was the girl you intended to marry. You never let me believe otherwise. If Lily would have had you, you would never have seriously considered me!'

'Gay——' He hesitated, ghastly pale, biting back the words which had involuntarily sprung to his llips. Sweat broke out on his broad forehead as he spoke others instead. 'I realise it looks bad . . .'

'The understatement of the year!' Gay was too hurt and furious to try and read between the lines. 'You picked me up and kissed me . . .'

'I wanted you!' he said hoarsely.

'Yes.' She felt herself flush all over even at the thought. 'So what?'

Luke's face went hard at her unconcealed mockery. 'I still want you.'

'You were obviously shocked when you discovered I was the maid,' she veered irrationally.

'I had the impression you were having an affair with Douglas,' he grated. 'Perhaps that's what shocked me.'

'What right had you to sit in judgment on me,' Gay cried, her blue eyes hotly indignant, 'when you openly confessed you were merely marrying to enhance your own image?'

Luke winced as though she had struck him. 'Yes,' he agreed flatly, 'it was in my mind.'

'It wasn't just in your mind!' Gay retorted fiercely. 'You were determined to marry Miss Dalmonte.'

Luke's strained silence, the terse set of his mouth, confirmed this so excruciatingly that Gay actually shuddered. She was as pale as he was now and she wished she could stop shivering.

Seeing it, he grasped her shoulders, his hands warm and insistent through her dress. 'Gay, why must we torture each other like this? You love me—I certainly care for you. Oh, God!' he drew her closer, bending his lips to her averted cheek, 'don't turn away from me now, my darling. I can't bear it.'

The feel of his mouth on her face almost proved her undoing. His hard male body pressed sensuously against her brought all her deepest emotions flaring into life. Yet strangely enough on this occasion the hurt in her mind was stronger than her physical feelings, so she was able to exercise some control.

'Yes,' she admitted, 'I did love you, Luke,' let him torture himself with that, in future, 'but I don't any more. I think I'd have died for you once,' she continued, with a glorious, unforgiving bitterness. 'Knowing you were with Lily hurt so much I couldn't sleep.'

'Gay!' he interposed, his voice so tortured she faltered, but not for long.

'How do you think I felt,' she rushed on heedlessly, 'when you decided, after Lily dropped you, that I would do? Not that you decided that until you discovered who my parents were. You made no effort to find me after she finished with you, did you? If you hadn't come to that reception I'd never have heard of you again!'

Luke might have been made of stone as her young anger flayed him. 'Don't think of it,' he begged hoarsely. 'You'll soon forget.'

That he made no real attempt to defend himself made him appear curiously worse in her eyes. 'How are the mighty fallen,' she quoted with a sneer. 'You're so determined to marry well that I think you'd be prepared to go down on your knees. You must be one of the biggest cheats I've ever met!'

'Gay!' he exclaimed savagely. 'Listen to me, for heaven's sake!'

'I won't—I——' Suddenly to her great consternation, she burst into tears. 'Oh, go away!' she cried helplessly.

His breath dragging, he ignored her outburst. Instead of doing as she asked, he gathered her close again, as if consoling her was more important than anything else. 'Don't thrash yourself like this, Gay. Let's start afresh.'

'Never!' she gasped.

He buried his face against her gleaming head and groaned. 'You're torturing both of us, darling.'

She tried to push him away. 'I'm not your darling!'

Still muttering hoarsely, he stared into the tear-drenched eyes she raised to his face, then, as if he couldn't help himself, he lowered his mouth and kissed her. Instantly between them passion flamed, a searing flame difficult to put out.

'Gay!' he gasped, as her lips parted, and she felt his body twist and jerk as if he, too, felt the flick of fire.

'No . . .!' As her mouth began searching wantingly for a deeper contact with his, and the room began spinning in dizzying glory, she managed, with her last ounce of willpower, to escape. 'It—it won't work, Luke,' she gulped, 'I hate you touching me!'

For a moment he appeared ready to take her and hold her by force, then his face hardened, draining of its brief flush of colour, leaving him white. 'You're still engaged to me, Gay.'

'A mockery.' Her voice shook.

'If it has to be,' he agreed grimly.

She noticed, with a cold feeling in the pit of her stomach, that he wasn't arguing any more. 'A few weeks, at the most.'

'I won't stay,' his eyes lingered with a curious hunger on her fresh young beauty, 'I don't think there's much point, not in the mood you're in. If I give you time to think you might realise nothing was ever gained by continually dragging up the past.'

'You always did,' she retorted, something driving her on. 'You were forever reminding me I was too free with men and not good enough for you.'

'All right, Gay,' his face etched in deep lines, he paused as he turned at the door, 'I get the message. I won't bother you any longer. All I ask is that we stick together for a week or two. Otherwise your mother is going to feel terribly guilty about accepting the car.'

It was a strange but quite valid reason for prolonging their engagement, so Gay agreed, but the next few weeks seemed the longest she had ever spent. She seldom saw Luke, and while she knew hopelessly that his absence caused her more pain than pleasure, she wasn't prepared for the agony which his announcement that he was going abroad for a month brought.

'This should give you time to think things over,' he said coolly, calling her from his office.

'I won't change my mind,' she replied stubbornly, disregarding every protesting inch of her body.

'Well, I won't try and change it for you,' he rejoined tightly.

'You couldn't!'

'Do you really believe I couldn't if I tried?' he asked mockingly. While she gasped, he enquired, 'Are you coming to the airport to see me off?'

'No, I am not!' she muttered, longing to.

'As you like,' he snapped coldly. 'There are others who might be more obliging. Perhaps it's just as well if you didn't see me off, anyway, as this seems the end of the road for us, I'm afraid.'

He sounded so final Gay shivered and went cold. She didn't think she could feel any colder until she saw a photograph of Luke with Lily Dalmonte at the airport. It was in the morning paper. They were smiling at each other and she had her hand on his arm. The caption ran: Is it a case of off with the new and back to the old for leading industrialist Luke Ashley?

Fiercely Gay screwed the paper up and threw it away before she could look at it again. Rent with a peculiar anger and pain, she almost didn't answer when the telephone rang. To her utter surprise it was Lily Dalmonte.

'I'd like to speak to you, please,' Lily Dalmonte asked quietly, after the briefest formalities had been exchanged. 'It's very important.'

About to refuse outright, Gay paused, anger giving way before an overwhelming desire to satisfy a painful curiosity. What did Lily want to see her about? Did she want to assure her she was willing to take Luke back? Her pictured face at the airport betrayed that she felt more for Luke than mere friendship. And what of him? Knowing she couldn't bear waiting until he returned to hear the truth, Gay capitulated. Suddenly she was heedless of the pride which these days consumed her.

Lily Dalmonte answered the door herself and took Gay quickly inside. In the lounge of the luxurious flat which Lily's father provided for her, the two girls faced each other guardedly.

Lily spoke first, and Gay couldn't help but admire the other girl's frankness. 'I saw Luke at the airport yesterday. I realised you weren't there and went to speak to him. I don't think he's happy. That's why I had to see you.'

Gay found herself flinching, not having expected anything quite so outspoken. Sharply she exclaimed, her face paling. 'I don't know why you should imagine the way he looked at the airport had anything to do with me. Or that it's any of your business. You gave him up . . .'

'Whoever told you that?' Lily intervened, frowning.

'Well, didn't you?' It was Gay's turn to frown and look uncertain.

Lily laughed, a curt sound. 'Do you really believe I would, given the choice? No, it was Luke who gave me up. Didn't he tell you?'

Stunned, Gay could only shake her head numbly.

Lily continued, the dull tone of her voice betraying that she no longer cared what she said. 'I thought we would be married. Oh, he hadn't actually proposed, but I knew he was leading up to it. He took me out and I never tried to hide how I felt about him. I couldn't understand why he hesitated. Then one day he went shopping with me, at Alice Farr's boutique in the King's Road. Something happened there—exactly what, I was never quite sure, but when I glanced at him his face was grey, which was definitely unusual for Luke. Something—someone, had given him a hell of a shock. That evening when, as arranged, we dined out, he told me he loved someone else.'

'I'm sorry,' Gay whispered, almost too stunned for words. She felt sick and shaken.

'I realised it was you, of course,' Lily sighed, 'when your engagement was announced, but yesterday Luke didn't have the appearance of being a happily engaged man. You weren't with him, and one or two things he said made me wonder, as well. I have nothing to lose,' she finished bitterly, 'so I decided to be brave—impertinent, if you like—and ask how things stood between you.'

'You—you mean you would still be prepared to marry him?' Gay stared at the other girl's haunted face, knowing she had been wrong about a lot of things. Lily Dalmonte was far from the grasping person she had imagined. She was mature, charming and beautiful. How could Luke ever have given her up?

'Yes,' Lily answered Gay bleakly, 'I still love him. I'd marry him tomorrow if I thought you didn't want him any more. If it were possible.'

'Perhaps he doesn't want me any more!' Gay cried. 'In fact, I'm almost sure he doesn't.' Blindly she turned and stumbled from the flat before a startled Lily could prevent her.

On reaching home, in the seclusion of her own room, Gay broke down completely. Throwing herself on her bed, she buried her hot face in the pillows. Why had Luke allowed her to believe Lily had given him up? There was no doubt in Gay's mind that the other girl loved him. It must have taken something very powerful to persuade Luke she wasn't for him. Gay tried to stop sobbing in an effort to think more clearly. Why, if Luke had discovered he loved her after seeing her at the boutique, hadn't he come after her immediately, or, if this hadn't been possible, sought her out later? Nothing made sense. That they had eventually met again appeared to have had more to do with providence than any particular effort on his part. Feeling exhausted and taut with despair, Gay drew a trembling breath. One thing was very obvious—everything was over between them; he had made that very clear. She had lost his love through her own stupid intolerance, and if Lily did win him back, she had no one but herself to blame.

The days which followed seemed so long, Gay never knew how she got through them, and when she tried to visualise a lifetime without Luke she couldn't face it. She couldn't sleep or eat, and she grew pale and listless. She was in such a state of torment, she began doing foolish things, without being wholly aware often of what she was doing. Nearing the end of the third week of Luke's absence, she was startled to find herself in the lift, going up to his office. Her parents were in Paris, and a sudden intolerable longing to hear Luke's name on someone's lips must have driven her unconsciously to seek out Miss Carson.

Miss Carson was busy and extremely surprised to see her. 'Mr Ashley isn't here, Miss Fenton, but surely you knew? He isn't due back for at least another week.'

'You're wrong about that,' said a light voice behind them, 'I got in over an hour ago.'

Startled, both Gay and Miss Carson turned, to find Luke standing in the doorway, tall and leanly elegant in a well tailored suit. His face was expressionless, but his grey eyes were dark as they rested on Gay and a nerve jerked at the side of his mouth before he controlled it. Then his glance slid from Gay to Miss Carson and he smiled briefly.

Gay tried to speak, but her head was swimming and her throat locked convulsively.

Luke turned back to her as she made an inarticulate little sound. 'I was going to call,' he said coldly, taking hold of her arm, as she appeared about to pass out. 'Is something wrong, Gay? What on earth brought you here?'

What indeed! Because she still found it impossible to speak, she stared at him, with a kind of trembling hopelessness that had his eyes suddenly narrowing warily. 'Come,' he commanded, shaking his head curtly as Miss Carson nervously suggested coffee. 'Later.'

Taking Gay through to his own office, he firmly closed the door on Miss Carson's curious face. Still watching Gay steadily, he told her to sit down. 'I'm not about to eat you,' he drawled cynically, as she obeyed with a shrinking movement he obviously mistook for fear. 'I got through quicker than I expected and decided to come home, that's all.'

'Why?' Gay found her voice at last, even if it was strained and low. A man like Luke didn't miscalculate by a week. There had to be a reason why he'd hurried home. She tried not to stare at him but failed. Her eyes seemed bent on devouring him, as though they hadn't seen him in years.

'Why?' he repeated, almost savagely. 'To end our farce of an engagement, if you like. I've had time to think, to realise it was a mistake to tie you down.'

Gay clenched her hands, in an effort to endure the pain his words inflicted. It had to come, of course. He was trying to be gallant, but his encounter with Lily at the airport was clearly behind such a decision.

She sat motionless, staring at him with wide, frightened eyes, trying desperately to think. 'Luke,' she faltered, feeling somehow that she was fighting for her very life, 'I've—I've seen Lily Dalmonte. She told me it was you who left her. Why did you let me believe it was the other way round . . .?'

For a long moment, after her voice trailed off unhappily, he was silent, then his mouth tightened. 'How did you happen to see her?' he asked carefully, without answering Gay's question, or confirming what she said.

'She rang——' Gay hesitated, wishing feverishly now that she hadn't said anything. 'I—I'd just been looking at your photograph in the morning paper, the one of you taken together at Heathrow, when she rang and asked me around to her flat.'

'And?' Luke prompted tonelessly.

'I didn't want to go, but I did—and she—she told me,' Gay explained incoherently.

'So?' Luke's shoulders lifted indifferently.

Surprisingly, Gay felt temper lending strength to her shaking limbs. 'Is that all you can say?' she choked. 'All this time you've let me believe it was Lily who gave you up. You should have told me the truth!'

His eyes glinted. 'I think we might both have benefited by following such advice.'

'Yes.' Gay hung her head to hide the anguished tears in her eyes as suddenly all the fight went out of her again. 'Oh, Luke, I've been much worse than you, though. I've thought such terrible things—while all along I've loved you desperately. It doesn't seem to make sense . . .'

'Gay, come here!' Swiftly he reached down to lift her from her chair. Setting her on her feet, he kept his arms around her, pulling her closer. As his arms tightened and his hands crushed her fragile bones, he groaned, 'Oh, God, you've gone so thin!'

'I—I haven't been able to eat,' she whispered, trembling, trying to stop herself clinging to him.

Bending his head, he spoke thickly against her cheek. 'Thank you for telling me you love me. I think I've loved you from the beginning. My attention was caught the first time I saw you, a slip of a girl with a cloud of the most beautiful hair, walking gracefully along the road. Not only that, I felt as though I'd been struck by electricity as soon as I spoke to you. It was unbelievable, I told myself it was crazy, but I couldn't get you out of my head.'

'Me neither,' Gay murmured incoherently.

He began kissing her almost savagely, then suddenly stopped. 'My behaviour has been regrettable, darling. I'd better try and explain. Having you in my head was bad enough, but when you began invading my heart I thought it was time to retreat. I did my best to hate you. I almost fell over myself to believe the worst of you. I welcomed every black mark I thought I'd found against your character, like a man gathering evidence to strengthen his defence.'

Anxiously Gay shook her head, somehow not able to bear seeing him so humble. 'Can't we forget the past, Luke? It doesn't seem to matter any more.'

'It does.' She saw his face was grim, the muscles tense along the hardness of his jaw. 'You see, I had my life completely mapped out. I intended marrying well, probably because of my lowly origins, but the notion was so deeply ingrained as to be almost immovable. To begin with, I imagined there would be little danger if I only saw you occasionally, but I soon realised I was mistaken. I tried ignoring you completely and concentrating on Lily. I was convinced I would forget you, but I didn't. The day I saw you at the boutique, I felt as though I'd been hit in the middle by a sledgehammer.'

'I felt the same way,' Gay faltered.

Kissing her again, Luke pulled her down with him, in the chair he had just lifted her out of. Cradling her to him, he took her mouth, parting her lips to his kisses. As her hands went around his neck, his fingers slid gently from her face to close possessively over the soft curve of her breast. 'I want you,' he groaned, against the warmth of her mouth. 'I wanted you then, you'll never know how much. I still remember the torture of that moment in that damned boutique. You floored me with a single glance. I knew then I was no use to Lily, or she to me.'

'But you didn't come after me,' Gay reminded him.

'No,' he agreed heavily, his eyes bleak, as they met her bewildered ones. 'I wanted to, but I had to tell Lily first. I knew I owed it to her. We had a date for dinner that evening and it seemed the least I could do, not to let her down. I'm afraid I'd led her to believe I was serious about her, although I'd never actually put anything in words. It wasn't easy, but we parted friends, but I never saw her again until I bumped into her at the airport. Nevertheless, I felt it was the least I could do to let people think she'd given me up.'

'I wish you'd told me,' Gay whispered. 'I've been so miserable.'

'I could have done,' he admitted heavily. 'I suppose it

was my pride, as much as anything else, that got in the way. You seemed to have such a low opinion of me.' He searched her face, his grey eyes suddenly tortured, 'If you've suffered, it's nothing to what I have. It's been hell these last few weeks without you. I meant to release you from our engagement because I thought you wanted to be free—not because I wanted to marry someone else.'

'I'm sorry, Luke,' she avoided his eyes. 'It seems I've misjudged you completely. I don't suppose you want to marry me now . . .'

'Just try and stop me!' He bent to her mouth again, but withdrew with a jerk, as though suddenly mindful of where he was and not able to trust himself completely. 'My God,' he muttered, 'I suffered agony searching London for you while all the time you were in Paris. I didn't connect that boutique in the King's Road with the kind of shop I imagined you worked in, or I might have found you sooner. It seemed a stroke of sheer luck when I found you as I did.'

Gay sighed, still able to shiver whenever she thought of their strange reunion. 'I got such a shock—I thought I was going crazy.'

'I didn't get that impression,' he rejoined grimly. 'You looked so cool I thought you wanted nothing more to do with me. But I knew I still wanted you,' he added darkly, his arms hurting. 'I loved you and meant to have you, no matter how I managed it. And,' he finished, with a touch of hurt reproach which she found strangely endearing, 'right up to that moment, all the time I'd been searching for you, to ask you to be my wife, I'd no idea who your parents were.'

'So you were prepared to take on an aggravating little nobody?' she teased, unsteadily.

'I only prayed she'd be willing to take me.'

'Yet you were so angry when you arrived at the cottage.'

'I was almost out of my mind,' he replied with dignity.

'I could have killed you for what you were putting me through, but it almost killed me when I nearly lost you in the river. You've no idea how I felt when I saw you disappearing under all that water. I certainly never want to feel like that again.'

As if attempting to erase the hurt she had caused him, Gay slid her arms around him and snuggled close. Turning her head against the broadness of his chest, she asked hesitantly, 'While we were at the cottage, Luke, you kissed me. You must have known what effect that had on me, yet you never tried to make love to me properly.' Her cheeks hot, she forced herself to continue. 'I've had no experience, I've never let any man go beyond a few kisses, yet if you'd persisted, I don't think I could have resisted you.'

He muttered something, his arms tightening, his face filled with a kind of savage exultation. Then he lifted her chin with gentle fingers, so he could read the clear innocence in her wide blue eyes. His voice, rough with emotion, he replied, 'I know now, but I didn't realise then, that you've never slept with any man. I thought you had affairs with them, then lost interest. I believed that if I made love to you, you would never marry me either. That,' he confessed with a harsh sigh, 'was why I didn't, but you'll never know how much I was tempted.'

'I would never deliberately tempt you, darling,' Gay smiled demurely, her pulses racing, weak with longing as she pressed against him.

'No?' Regaining something of his old authority, Luke's dark brows rose quizzically as he trapped her roaming hands with one of his. 'Just what do you think you're doing now? Don't tell me you have no idea. I refuse to believe,' his glance swept her flushed face with mock severity, 'you're as innocent as all that.'

Not daring to deny it and only half aware of what she was doing, Gay freed a hand and curled it around his neck, drawing his mouth down to her own. 'I love you,' she breathed, as he began kissing her deeply and passionately.

'Which might just about excuse you,' he muttered against her lips, his mouth weaving spells while his hands caressed the swelling curves of her body. 'I adore you,' he said.

Some time later he reluctantly broke his embrace as a tentative knock came to the door. As he stared down at Gay's drowsy blue eyes, his voice thickened. 'We'd better get out of here, my darling, before we completely offend poor Miss Carson's sensibilities.'

'Where will we go?' Half lost in the wave of excitement sweeping through her, dazed from the promise of ecstasy to come, Gay didn't much care.

'Go?' Luke's eyes darkened. 'I'd like to take you back to my place, but it might be safer to wait until we're married.'

'When will we be?' Colour stole in to her face as she asked the question, but she was eager to know.

'Soon.' He rose to his feet, still holding her tightly, and she could feel his heart beating heavily. 'I made all the arrangements weeks ago and they've never been cancelled. All there's left for you to decide is the honeymoon.'

'Why . . .!' she began, only to find her pretended indignation smothered under his demanding mouth. Minutes later, as they went down in the lift, she recalled how differently she had felt an hour ago. Then she had been so unhappy she hadn't wanted to go on living. Now everything was changed. Luke loved her and they were soon to be married.

'Oh, Luke,' she smiled tremulously, 'I came here because I was desperate to hear someone speak your name. I went to see Miss Carson with that in mind, but I had really no idea what I was going to say to her. I was so lonely for you . . .'

Luke's voice was gently teasing as he answered, but his eyes were warm with love. 'Never mind, my darling,

I can guarantee you won't have to do without me again, not ever!'

His words were so alive with promise that Gay was content, and the smile she gave him was adoring as he took her hand and together they walked out into the summer sunshine.

Harlequin Plus

A WORD ABOUT THE AUTHOR

Margaret Pargeter was born in the quiet Northumbrian Valley, in the extreme northeast of England, where she lives today.

When did she first feel an urge to write? "Truthfully, I can't recall," she admits. "It must have been during my early teens. I remember carrying a notebook in my pocket, and while milking cows I would often take a break to scribble something down."

The jottings developed into short stories, and Margaret's first break came several years after she had married. Her husband talked her into entering a writing contest, and her work caught the eye of an editor, who asked her to write serial stories. From there she went on to complete her first romance novel, *Winds from the Sea* (Romance #1899).

Among the author's many blessings, which she likes to keep counting, is the "pleasure I get from knowing that people enjoy reading my books. And," she adds, "I hope they long continue to do so."